HOW IT ENDED

JAY McINERNEY

BLOOMSBURY

For Julian

First published in Great Britain 2000
This paperback edition published 2001

Bloomsbury Publishing Plc, 38 Soho Square, London W1D 3HB

A CIP catalogue record for this book
is available from the British Library

ISBN 0 7475 5356 4

10 9 8 7 6 5 4 3 2

The stories in this book were previously published as follows:

The Atlantic Monthly: 'Smoke'; *Esquire:* 'Reunion'; *Granta:* 'The Business' and
'Getting in Touch with Lonnie'; *Playboy:* 'Con Doctor' and 'How It Ended'.
'The Queen and I' was originally published in *Spin* and as a Bloomsbury Quid
paperback original by Bloomsbury Publishing Plc.

Typeset by Palimpsest Book Production Limited,
Polmont, Stirlingshire

Printed in England by Clays Ltd, St Ives plc

'And anything that ever happened to me after
   I never felt the same about again.'

   – Frank O'Connor, 'Guests of the Nation'

CONTENTS

THIRD PARTY

DIFFICULT TO DESCRIBE PRECISELY, the taste of that eighth or ninth cigarette of the day, a mix of ozone, blond tobacco and early-evening angst on the tongue. But he recognized it every time. It was the taste of lost love.

Alex started smoking again whenever he lost a woman. When he fell in love again he would quit. And when love died, he'd light up again. Partly it was a physical reaction to stress; partly metaphorical – the substitution of one addiction for another. And no small part of this reflex was mythological – indulging a romantic image of himself as a lone figure standing on a bridge in a foreign city, cigarette cupped in his hand, his leather jacket open to the elements.

He imagined the passersby speculating about his private sorrow as he stood on the Pont des Arts, mysterious, wet and unapproachable. His sense of loss seemed more real when he imagined himself through the eyes of strangers. The pedestrians with their evening baguettes and their Michelin guides and their umbrellas, hunched against the March precipitation, an alloy of drizzle and mist.

When it all ended with Lydia he'd decided to go to Paris, not only because it was a good place to smoke, but because it seemed like the appropriate backdrop. His grief was more poignant and picturesque in that city. Bad enough that Lydia had left him; what made it worse was that it was his own fault; he suffered both the ache of the victim and the guilt of the villain. His appetite had not suffered, however; his stomach was complaining like a terrier demanding its evening walk, blissfully unaware that the household was in mourning. Ennobling as it might seem to suffer in Paris, only a fool would starve himself there.

Standing in the middle of the river he tried to decide which way to go. Having dined last night in a bistro that looked grim and authentic enough for his purposes but which proved to be full of voluble Americans and Germans attired as if for the gym or the tropics, he decided to head for the Hôtel Coste, where, at the very least, the Americans would be fashionably jaded and dressed in shades of gray and black.

The bar was full and, of course, there were no tables when he arrived. The hostess, a pretty Asian sylph with a West London accent, sized him up skeptically. Hers was not the traditional Parisian hauteur, the sneer of the *maître d'hôtel* at a three-star restaurant; she was rather the temple guardian of that international tribe which included rock stars, fashion models, designers, actors and directors – as well as those who photographed them, wrote about them, and fucked them. As the art director of a boutique ad agency, Alex lived on the fringes of this world. In New York he knew many of the doormen and *maître d's*, but here the best he could hope was that he looked the part. The hostess seemed to be puzzling over his claims to membership; her expression slightly hopeful, as if she was on the verge of giving him the benefit of the doubt. Suddenly her narrow squint gave way to a smile of recognition. 'I'm sorry, I didn't recognize you,' she said. 'How are you?' Alex had only been here twice, on a visit a few years before; it seemed unlikely he would have been remembered. On the other hand, he was a generous tipper and, he reasoned, not a bad-looking guy.

She led him to a small but highly visible table set for four. He'd told her he was expecting someone in the hopes of increasing his chances of seating. 'I'll send a waiter right over,' she said. 'Let me know if there's anything else I can do for you.' So benevolent was her smile that he tried to think of some small request to gratify her.

Still feeling expansive when the waiter arrived, he ordered a bottle of champagne. He scanned the room. While he recognized several of the patrons – a burly American novelist of the Montana school, the skinny lead singer of a Brit Pop band – he didn't see anyone he actually *knew* in the old-fashioned sense. Feeling self-conscious in his solitude, he studied the menu and wondered why he'd never brought Lydia to Paris. He regretted it now, for her sake as well as his own; the pleasures of travel were less real to him when they couldn't be verified by a witness.

He'd taken her for granted – that was part of the problem. Why did that always happen?

When he looked up a young couple was standing at the edge of the room, searching the crowd. The woman was striking – a tall beauty of indeterminate race. They seemed

5

disoriented, as if they had been summoned to a brilliant party which had migrated elsewhere. The woman met his gaze – and smiled. Alex smiled back. She tugged on her companion's sleeve and nodded toward Alex's table.

Suddenly they were approaching.

'Do you mind if we join you for a moment,' the woman asked. 'We can't find our friends.' She didn't wait for the answer, taking the seat next to Alex, exposing, in the process, a length of taupe-colored, unstockinged thigh.

'Frederic,' the man said, extending his hand. He seemed more self-conscious than his companion. 'And this is Tasha.'

'Please, sit,' Alex said. Some instinct prevented him from giving his own name.

'What are *you* doing in Paris?' Tasha asked.

'Just, you know, getting away.'

The waiter arrived with the champagne.

Alex requested two more glasses.

'I think we have some friends in common,' Tasha said. 'Ethan and Frederique.'

Alex nodded noncommittally.

'I love New York,' Frederic said.

'It's not what it used to be,' Tasha countered.

'I know what you mean.' Alex wanted to see where this was going.

'Still,' Frederic said, 'it's better than Paris.'

'Well,' Alex said. 'Yes and no.'

'Barcelona,' Frederic said, 'is the only hip city in Europe.'

'And Berlin,' said Tasha.

'Not any more.'

'Do you know Paris well,' Tasha asked.

'Not really.'

'We should show you.'

'It's shit,' Frederic said.

'There are some new places,' she said, 'that aren't too boring.'

'Where are *you* from?' Alex asked the girl, trying to parse her exotic looks.

'I live in Paris,' she said.

'When she's not in New York.'

They drank the bottle of champagne and ordered another. Alex was happy for the company. Moreover he couldn't help liking himself as whomever they imagined him to be. The idea that they had mistaken him for someone else was tremendously liberating. And he was fascinated by Tasha, who was definitely flirting with him. Several times she grabbed his knee for emphasis and at several points she scratched her left breast. An absent-minded gesture, or a deliberately provocative one? Alex tried to determine if her attachment to Frederic was romantic. The signs pointed in both directions. The Frenchman watched her closely and yet he didn't seem to resent her flirting. At one point she said, 'Frederic and I used to go out.' The more Alex looked at her the more enthralled he became. She was a perfect cocktail of racial features, familiar enough to answer an acculturated ideal and exotic enough to startle.

'You Americans are so puritanical,' she said. 'All this fuss about your president getting a blow job.'

'It has nothing to do with sex,' Alex answered, conscious of a flush rising on his cheeks. 'It's a right-wing coup.' He'd wanted to sound cool and jaded. Yet somehow it came out defensive.

'Everything has to do with sex,' she said, staring into his eyes.

Thus provoked, the Veuve Cliquot tingling like a brilliant isotope in his veins, he ran his hand up the inside of her thigh, stopping only at the border of her tight short skirt. Holding his gaze, she opened her mouth with her tongue and moistened her lips.

'This is shit,' said Frederic.

Although Alex was certain the other man couldn't see his hand the subject of Frederic's exclamation was worrisomely indeterminate.

'You think everything is shit.'

'That's because it is.'

'You're an expert on shit.'

'There's no more art. Only shit.'

'Now that *that*'s settled,' said Tasha.

A debate about dinner: Frederic wanted to go to Buddha Bar, Tasha wanted to stay. They compromised, ordering caviar and another bottle of champagne. When the check arrived Alex remembered at the last moment not to throw down his credit card. He decided, as a first step toward elucidating the mystery of his new identity, that he was the kind of guy who paid cash. While Alex counted out the bills Frederic gazed studiously into the distance with the air of a man who is practiced in the art of ignoring checks. Alex had a brief, irritated intuition that he was being used. Maybe this was a routine with them, pretending to recognize a stranger with a good table. Before he could develop this notion Tasha had taken his arm and was leading him out into the night. The pressure of her arm, the scent of her skin, were invigorating. He decided to see where this would take him. It wasn't as if he had anything else to do.

Frederic's car, which was parked a few blocks away, did not look operational. The front grill was bashed in; one of the headlights pointed up at a forty-five degree angle. 'Don't worry,' Tasha said. 'Frederic's an excellent driver. He only crashes when he feels like it.'

'How are you feeling *tonight?*' Alex asked.

'I feel like dancing,' he said. He began to sing Bowie's 'Let's Dance', drumming his hands on the steering wheel as Alex climbed into the back.

Le Bain Douche was half empty. The only person they recognized was Bernard Henri Levy. Either they were too early, or a couple of years too late. The conversation had lapsed into French and Alex wasn't following everything. Tasha was all over him, stroking his arm and, intermittently, her own perfect left breast, and he was a little nervous about Frederic's reaction. At one point there was a sharp exchange which he didn't catch. Frederic stood up and walked off.

'Look,' Alex said. 'I don't want to cause any trouble.'

'No trouble,' she said.

'Is he your boyfriend?'

'We used to go out. Now we're just friends.'

She pulled him forward and kissed him, slowly exploring the inside of his mouth with her tongue. Suddenly she leaned away and glanced up at a woman in a white leather jacket who was dancing beside an adjoining table.

'I think big tits are beautiful,' she said before kissing him with renewed ardor.

'I think *your* tits are beautiful,' he said.

'They are, actually,' she said. 'But not big.'

When Frederic returned his mood seemed to have lifted. He laid several bills on the table. 'Let's go,' he said.

Alex hadn't been clubbing in several years. After he and Lydia had moved in together the clubs had lost their appeal. Now he felt the return of the old thrill, the anticipation of the hunt – the sense that the night held secrets which would be unveiled before it was over. Tasha was talking about someone in New York that Alex was supposed to know. 'The last time I saw him he just kept banging his head against the wall, and I said to him, Michael, you've really got to stop doing these drugs. It's been fifteen years now.'

First stop was a ballroom in Montmartre. A band was onstage playing an almost credible version of 'Smells Like Teen Spirit'. While they waited at the bar, Frederic played vigorous air guitar and shouted the refrain, 'Here we are now, entertain us.' After sucking down their cosmopolitans they drifted out to the dance floor. The din was just loud enough to obviate conversation.

The band launched into 'Goddamn the Queers'. Tasha divided her attentions between the two of them, grinding her pelvis into Alex during a particularly bad rendition of 'Champagne SuperNova'. Closing his eyes and enveloping her with his arms, he lost track of his spatial co-ordinates. Were those her breasts, or the cheeks of her ass in his hands? She flicked her tongue in his ear; he pictured a cobra rising from a wicker basket.

When he opened his eyes he saw Frederic and another man conferring and watching him from the edge of the dance floor.

Alex went off to find the Men's Room and another beer. When he returned, Tasha and Frederic were slow-dancing to a French ballad and making out. He decided to leave and cut his losses. Whatever the game was, he suddenly felt too tired to play it. At that moment Tasha looked across the room and waved to him from the dance floor. She slalomed toward him through the dancers, Frederic following behind her.

'Let's go,' she shouted.

Out on the sidewalk, Frederic turned obsequious. 'Man, you must think Paris is total shit.'

'I'm having a good time,' Alex said. 'Don't worry about it.'

'I do worry about it, man. It's a question of *honor*.'

'I'm fine.'

'At least we could find some drugs,' said Tasha.

'The drugs in Paris are all shit.'

'I don't need drugs,' Alex said.

'*Don't want to get stoned,*' Frederic sang. '*But I don't want to not get stoned.*'

They began to argue about the next destination. Tasha was making the case for a place called, apparently, Faster Pussycat, Kill Kill. Frederic insisted it wasn't open. He was pushing L'Enfer. The debate continued in the car. Eventually they crossed the river and later still lurched to a stop beneath the Montparnasse tower.

The two doormen greeted his companions warmly. They

descended the staircase into a space which seemed to glow with a purple light, the source of which Alex could not discern. A throbbing drum and bass riff washed over the dancers. Grabbing hold of the tip of his belt, Tasha led him toward a raised area above the dance floor which seemed to be a VIP area.

Conversation became almost impossible. Which was kind of a relief. Alex met several people, or rather, nodded at several people who in turn nodded at him. A Japanese woman shouted into his ear in what was probably several languages and later returned with a catalogue of terrible paintings. He nodded as he thumbed through the catalogue. Apparently it was a gift. Far more welcome – a man handed him an unlabeled bottle full of clear liquid. He poured some into his glass. It tasted like moonshine.

Tasha towed him out to the dance floor. She wrapped her arms around him and sucked his tongue into her mouth. Just when his tongue felt like it was going to be ripped from his mouth she bit down on it, hard. Within moments he tasted blood. Perhaps this was what she wanted, for she continued to kiss him as she thrust her pelvis into his. She sucked hard on his tongue. He imagined himself sucked whole into her mouth. He liked the idea. And without for a moment losing his focus on Tasha, he suddenly thought of Lydia and the girl before Lydia, and the girl after Lydia, the one he had betrayed her with. How was it, he wondered, that desire for one woman always reawakened his desire for all the other women in his life?

'Let's get out of here,' he shouted, mad with lust. She nodded and pulled away, going into a little solipsistic dance a few feet away. Alex watched, trying to pick and follow her rhythm until he gave up and captured her in his arms. He forced his tongue between her teeth, surprised by the pain of his recent wound. Fortunately she didn't bite him this time; in fact she pulled away. Suddenly she was weaving her way back to the VIP area, where Frederic seemed to be having an argument with the bartender. When he saw Tasha he seized a bottle on the bar and threw it at the floor near her feet, where it shattered.

Frederic shouted something unintelligible before bolting up the stairs. Tasha started to follow.

'Don't go,' Alex shouted, holding her arm.

'I'm sorry,' she shouted, removing his hand from her arm. She kissed him gently on the lips.

'Say goodbye,' Alex said.

'Goodbye.'

'Say my name.'

She looked at him quizzically, and then, as if she suddenly got the joke, she smiled and laughed mirthlessly, pointing at him as if to say – you almost got me.

He watched her disappear up the steps, her long legs seeming to become even longer as they receded.

Alex had another glass of the clear liquor but the scene now struck him as tawdry and flat. It was a little past three. As he was leaving the Japanese woman pressed several nightclub invitations into his hand.

Out on the sidewalk he tried to get his bearings. He started to walk toward St Germain. His mood lifted with the thought that it was only ten o'clock in New York. He would call Lydia. Suddenly he believed he knew what to say to her. As he picked up his pace he noticed a beam of light moving slowly along the wall beside and above him; he turned to see Frederic's bashed-in Renault cruising the street behind him.

'Get in,' said Tasha.

He shrugged. Whatever happened, it was better than walking.

'Frederic wants to check out his after-hours place.'

'Maybe you could just drop me off at my hotel.'

'Don't be a drag.'

The look she gave him awoke in him the mad lust of the dance floor; he was tired of being jerked around and yet his desire overwhelmed his pride. After all this he felt he deserved his reward and he realized he was willing to do almost anything to get it. He climbed in the back seat. Frederic gunned the engine and popped the clutch. Tasha looked back at Alex, shaping her lips into a kiss, then turned to Frederic. Her tongue emerged from her lips and slowly disappeared in Frederic's ear. When Frederic stopped for a light she moved around to kiss him full on the mouth. Alex realized that he was involved – that he was part of the transaction between them. And suddenly he thought of Lydia, how he had told her his betrayal had nothing to do with her, which was what you said. How could he explain to her that as he bucked atop another woman it was she, Lydia, who filled his heart.

Tasha suddenly climbed over the back seat and started kissing him. Thrusting her busy tongue into his mouth, she ran her hand down to his crotch. 'Oh, yes, where did that come from?' She took his earlobe between her teeth as she unzipped his fly.

14

Alex moaned as she reached into his shorts. He looked at Frederic, who looked right back at him . . . who seemed to be driving faster as he adjusted the rear-view mirror. Tasha slid down his chest, feathering the hair of his belly with her tongue. A vague intuition of danger faded away in the wash of vivid sensation. She was squeezing his cock in her hand and then it was in her mouth and he felt powerless to intervene. He didn't care what happened, so long as she didn't stop. At first he could barely feel the touch of her lips, the pleasure residing more in the anticipation of what was to follow. At last she raked him gently with her teeth. Alex moaned and squirmed lower in the seat as the car picked up speed.

The pressure of her lips became more authoritative.

'Who am I?' he whispered. And a minute later: 'Tell me who you think I am.'

Her response, though unintelligible, forced a moan of pleasure from his own lips. Glancing at the rear-view mirror, he saw that Frederic was watching, looking down into the back seat, even as the car picked up speed. When Frederic shifted abruptly into fourth, Alex inadvertently bit down on his own tongue as his head snapped forward, his teeth scissoring the fresh wound there.

On a sudden impulse he pulled out of Tasha's mouth just as Frederic jammed on the brakes and sent them into a spin.

He had no idea how much time passed before he struggled out of the car. The crash had seemed almost leisurely, the car turning like a falling leaf until the illusion of weightlessness was shattered by the collision with the guardrail. He tried to remember it all as he sat, folded like a contortionist in the back seat, taking inventory of his extremities. A peaceful, Sunday silence prevailed. No one seemed to be moving. His cheek was sore and bleeding on the inside where he'd slammed it against the passenger-seat headrest. Just when he was beginning to suspect his hearing was gone he heard Tasha moaning beside him. The serenity of survival was replaced by anger when he saw Frederic's head moving on the dashboard and remembered what might have happened.

Hobbling around to the other side of the car, he yanked the door open and hauled Frederic roughly out to the pavement, where he lay blinking, a gash on his forehead.

'What was that about?' Alex said.

The Frenchman blinked and winced, inserting a finger in his mouth to check his teeth.

In a fury, Alex kicked him in the ribs. 'Who the hell do you think I am?'

Frederic smiled and looked up at him. 'You're just a guy,' he said. 'You're nobody.'

SIMPLE GIFTS

BY THE TIME THEY dropped her off at Irving Place it was nearly midnight. The Thruway from Buffalo had been harrowing. The van was barely roadworthy under the best of conditions; between the ice and the wind it was practically a miracle they'd made it home, especially when you considered that Lenny finally admitted somewhere around Utica that he'd dropped half a tab of acid. Rory had taken the other half, which disqualified him as a driver, and Zac had lost his license after the DUI in Cleveland, which left Lori as the only eligible pilot. Once again Lori was den mother to a trio of stoned scouts. *Backup:* wasn't that supposed to imply support, solidity, watching *her* back, if not massaging it on a nightly basis. When she'd hooked up with these guys she hadn't imagined that it meant carrying the amps and covering the licks which they were too stoned to remember.

She didn't think she'd ever been so tired in her whole life, between the drive and the partying last night, although the sight of the city had briefly revived her, the lights, the people, the improbable beauty of the snow on the streets.

'Hey, Merry Christmas, babe,' Rory said as he slid across the seat to take her place at the wheel. He reached out the window and slapped a foil packet in her hands.

She watched the wheels spin on the slick street as the van fishtailed up the street with its vanity plate: THE MAGI. They'd been the Magi before Lori hooked up with them – it turned out that Zac had been under the impression that it was the plural of *The Magus*, the title of a way cool novel his girlfriend had told him about which 'had this like Magician guy doing all this like crazy shit' – and since the band already had a local following they'd kept the name: Lori and the Magi.

Jeffrey was fooling with the lights on the Christmas tree when she came in. 'Jesus, I thought you died on the thruway.' She detected the note of petulance in his voice.

'Almost.'

Tired as she was she wanted to lift his mood; she bounded over and kissed him, tasting the sweet sour tang of whiskey on his breath.

'You know, until I was about twelve I thought all men smelled like Scotch. I thought it was a, whatdoyoucallit. Secondary sexual characteristic, like facial hair.'

'How are the three wise men? Following any stars tonight?'

'I just hope they can make it to Brooklyn.' She told the story of the trip – most of it, anyway – trying to strike a fine tonal balance between comedy and suspense.

'Jesus,' he said, 'when are you going to get rid of those clowns?' The Magi were a source of some friction in the household.

She kissed him again. 'As soon as you learn to play bass and drums.'

He turned away to adjust one of the lights on the tree. 'So how was the last gig?'

'I would have called,' she said. 'But I didn't want to wake you. Forty-two Buffalo Metalheads in a bar the size of our apartment.'

'How do they compare to Syracuse metalheads?'

'A little hairier, I think.'

'Ah, the glamour of the rock-and-roll life.'

'How's the play?'

'Incomprehensible. But the lighting is going to be a killer.'

She went into the kitchen and got a beer. 'I am so fucking beat,' she said.

'I was kind of hoping we could go out.'

'Out. Tonight?'

'I sort of felt like dancing.'

'Is this, like, a tradition in your family? Going out to a club on Christmas Eve?'

'It's my answer to midnight mass.'

It was their first Christmas together; they didn't yet have their own traditions. Well, why not dancing? Lori wanted to please him. He was practically the first guy she'd ever gone out with who wasn't a complete asshole. Or bi. Or a junkie. Who was in fact, so far as she could tell after six months, a great guy. Just as she was starting to make a name for herself singing songs about what creeps guys were, she'd gone and fallen in love. Hooked up with a lover and a band at almost the same moment.

As much as she wanted to sleep at this moment she was

conscious of the occasion. She liked to imagine they might be spending future Christmases together, so it seemed important to set the right precedents. He'd bought the tree and gone insane with the lights – it was his profession, after all. One of the first things she'd liked about him: *Lighting Designer*. The very concept – a man who taught light how to act. The places she played she felt lucky to get a spotlight. And the matter-of-fact way in which he said it, the way another guy would say *computer programmer*.

Seeing the lights and the wrapped presents beneath the tree, she suddenly felt terribly guilty.

'Is that really what you want to do? Go dancing?'

'Don't worry about it,' he said. 'It was just an idea.'

'It's not that I don't want to stay up with you,' she said, moving closer to him on the couch and kissing his ear. 'I think I could summon the energy to give you a special Christmas treat.'

'A treat? Could it be . . . the Vulcan mind meld?'

'It's not your mind I'm interested in.'

'That's good. For both our sakes.'

'Maybe a shower will revive me.'

'Don't worry about it. We can celebrate tomorrow.'

Jeffrey seemed sincere, but she felt terrible about disappointing him.

In the bedroom she lay down and dozed off almost immediately. Waking a few minutes later, she suddenly remembered the packet that Rory had given her. That was the answer. Jeffrey was so excited about their first Christmas together. She didn't want to let him down. Especially now. In Syracuse she'd seen an old lover, Will Porter. He'd come to the gig and she'd gone back to his apartment, after, ostensibly because he didn't like to hang out in bars. A year out of rehab, he suddenly appeared to be everything she had wished for back then. Was it possible to change that much?

Feeling a fresh stab of guilt, she fished the drugs out of her jeans and walked over to the dresser, opening the foil carefully, separating out two fat lines with a Metro card and rolling up a bill.

The first line almost took her head off. Jesus, she thought – it's *crank*. For some reason she'd assumed it was coke. Like who wouldn't. At first she was pissed and then she thought, what the fuck – if she wanted to stay up she might as well *stay up*. She could sleep tomorrow. In the meantime, Jeffrey had a dance partner. She did the other line for good measure, then stepped into the shower.

By the time she emerged she was up for anything, although she was a little too jumpy to give Jeffrey his blow job just yet. Right at this moment the idea seemed a little . . . nauseating. But now they had the whole night ahead of them. She changed into her black vinyl skirt and the pink spandex top she'd bought at Patricia Field for her gig at CBGBs.

Emerging into the living room, she found Jeffrey sitting on the floor in front of the TV watching *How the Grinch Stole Christmas*. She stole up behind and tackled him.

'Whoa, what's gotten into you?'

'It's just your rock-and-roll girl, ready to dance.'

He fended off her attack and held her at arm's length, looking into her eyes.

'Oh, my God. You're wired.'

'I wanted to stay up with my baby.'

'I don't believe this.'

'What's the matter?' She stopped wrestling with him. He'd never been judgmental about drugs before.

'You're fucking *wired*.'

'I left some for you if that's what you're worried about.'

'This is rich.'

'What's rich?'

He took her hands in his. 'You looked so tired and I felt so sorry for you.'

'I was.'

'I just took three halcyon.'

It took a moment for this dart to lodge itself in her speeding brain.

'Oh, shit.'

'Oh yeah.'

She began to laugh. She collapsed into his arm, laughing. 'Merry Christmas,' she said.

He kissed her. As much as she wanted to kiss him his lips felt strange on her own, which were slightly numb and which had begun to take on a life of their own.

He managed to stay awake for another half-hour, during which she regaled him with tales of upstate New York, and Toronto, the quirks of the locals and the outrages perpetrated by her band mates, until he began to nod off on the couch.

'I'm awake,' he said, several times, as he snapped his head upright. In the end she pulled off his shoes and put a quilt over him.

How was it that on this, the first promising Christmas

of her life, she ended up alone again. She tried to think of who she could call. Certainly not her parents, whom she hadn't spoken to in more than a year. She briefly considered calling Will Porter, her lost-and-found lover, who taught her how to play the blues like Bukka White and later how to live them. Waiting all night for him to come home, hiding her money in the toilet tank . . . that night dragging him into the bathtub and filling it with cold water and ice the way he told her. Will finally turning blue, if not black.

She was crying. To console herself she did another couple of lines, not that the first were wearing off, not that they wouldn't keep her buzzing into the dawn, but she wanted to get past the guilt about Will. She was entitled to that, surely, on a lonely Christmas Eve.

She called the loft in Brooklyn where the boys would be, but she only got the answering machine, which played a bar from the Sex Pistols' 'God Save the Queen'.

After watching *Carnal Knowledge* and sweeping the entire apartment, she tried to rouse Jeffrey, sleeping on the couch, a thin trail of saliva running down his cheek.

'Honey?' She shook his shoulder. 'Honey, are you awake?' She turned up the volume on the TV and then undid his belt and began to massage his cock. After a few minutes he shook his head and turned away from her, burying his face in the cushions. She scratched at the skin on her arms, tormented by an invisible rash. If only Jeffrey would wake up long enough to scratch her back.

On one of many circuits through the kitchen she decided to scrub the sink. She rubbed and polished until the green

Ajax slush and the pink sponge had both disappeared. Then she took an old toothbrush to the grout around the tiles. Jeffrey couldn't complain about her housekeeping when he woke up tomorrow. Afterwards she took the toothbrush to the elusive itch beneath the skin of her arms and her neck. Lighting a cigarette, she looked down into the shiny white sink with the sudden conviction that she would be sucked into the drain if she did not move away immediately. She backed away and lit a second cigarette from the first.

She walked back to the bedroom and looked out into the courtyard, counting the lighted windows, as she reached behind her shoulder to scratch her back. Twenty-three the first time she counted, twenty-four the second. As she watched, one third-floor window went dark. Walking back through the living room, past the Christmas tree, she stopped to look at the gifts under the tree. Five packages, plus a bottle of Cuervo Gold with a ribbon around it. His presents to her were wrapped up in pages from *Interview* magazine. The square box which she was pretty sure was a DAT recorder showed Chrissie Hynde's face. Looking at the presents she found herself remembering the Shaker hymn:

> *'Tis a gift to be simple*
> *'tis a gift to be free*
> *'tis a gift to come down*
> *Where we ought to be.*

That was all she could remember.

As she walked into the kitchen, she wondered where she

would be next Christmas, and with whom. She opened the refrigerator, although she had no desire to eat. Surely there was something she wanted to do, something that would fulfill this nameless compulsion, this desire without object.

Somehow it always ended up like this – solo at the edge of dawn. The stage was dark, the audience gone home. She tried to picture a lifetime of Christmases with Jeffrey and she could not. It wasn't his fault. It was her. The way she was. She shivered, feeling the chill from the open refrigerator on the prickly envelope of her skin. She tried to imagine herself rising away from her own skin and leaving it behind – like a snake's, like an empty shell of wrapping paper – lifting away from her old body, emerging strange and new.

That's what she really wanted to give him. A whole new girl.

'Wake up, honey,' she would say. 'It's Christmas.'

MY PUBLIC SERVICE

WAS IT KISSINGER WHO said power is aphrodisiac? The dictator with his cabaret dancer, the studio boss and the starlet, all the ruthless, puff-bellied, hairy-eared trolls with their creamy cupcakes; the desk-top couplings, the dribbling idolaters on their knees . . . it's hardly a notion to inspire poetry, or pride of species. But the quest for power can be a search for love. This is what occurs to me now, years after I helped bring the Senator down.

Like many before him he required women. It was a compulsion, like drinking for some men. He was a teetotaler, but he couldn't bear to pass a night alone. If he had fifteen minutes between appointments he wanted to spend it in hot congress with a warm body. One of my jobs was to summon them, smuggle them up the back stairs, through the rear door, spirit them out in the service elevator just ahead of his wife who'd taken the early flight. The blonde in the second row, the stewardess named Tami, the student who asked that interesting question about mental health. I would say, the Senator was very impressed with your X and would like to meet you in his room. Your question, your comment, your thoughts on the health-care question, your thorough and enlightening explanation of the safety features of the Boeing 747, your long blonde tresses, your tits. At first I was embarrassed. A former fat boy who retained the doughy, pig-gaited self-image long after the lard had melted away, I was nearly incapable of approaching women on my own behalf, but as the Senator's emissary, I'm ashamed to say I became good at putting just the right spin on these invitations: it was important that candidates understand it was not actually their opinions on the health-care question that were being solicited, the Senator not having time to waste on preliminaries, while it was also important to communicate all of this by implication, deniability being crucial in case the lady in question was unreceptive. I'm sorry to say there weren't many refusals.

There was a type: slim, no ass, big tits and long blonde hair. Not that he wouldn't compromise his standards in a pinch, politics being the art of compromise, after all.

And now that I have given you every reason to despise the man, let me tell you that I loved him, and I was one of many. The women weren't drugged, or coerced. Neither were the voters. In a democracy, seduction replaces rape. He was the most magnetic individual I have ever met. When I arrived on the Hill during the dark days of the Republican ascendancy, all the young Democrats wanted to work for Senator Castelton, the fresh-faced, sandy-haired Solon of his day. At that time he was becoming known as a champion of comprehensive national health care and tax reform. The press liked him because he was young and photogenic – the same reasons that they would later dislike him.

He came out of the high plains, his exact origins obscured in a cloud of red prairie dust and self-invention. (I myself am obscuring and changing, for obvious reasons.) The campaign biography stated that his father had died in combat in the Second World War. That was the start of the trouble, when an enterprising reporter found the birth certificate that listed Unknown as father. The fallout from this revelation was mixed, the Senator gaining perhaps as much sympathy for his fatherlessness as censure for his mendacity. After the first disclosure, the second-day press was somewhat cautious, accompanied by sidebars about compassionate man-on-the-street reaction and a smattering of breast-beating editorials about the role of the press. Subsequent revelations about his background – the mother's lack of visible means of support, the hospitalizations – were handled gingerly, almost apologetically. The Senator was perceived by many to be the double victim of an unfortunate childhood and an insensitive press. Trey Davis, the former administrative assistant who worked on the campaign, used to joke that the episode bought him an extra planeload of blondes.

The senator himself was reticent about his background and in the end I'm not sure he could separate his own inventions from the facts. But one day in Georgia, during his first presidential bid, he told me about his mother. He'd just addressed a group of students at a private university and had been confronted by a shouting delegation from a nearby bible college who denounced his opinions on school prayer and abortion. Standing up to the protestors, he called them narrow-minded religious bigots; the event had ended in an uproar with part of the audience chanting the Lord's Prayer to drown out the voice from the podium. Driving back to Atlanta he was seething. After many miles of silence he suddenly told me that his mother had been involved with a group called the Assemblies of God, to which she tithed much of what little money she was able to beg from relatives or collect from the state. His jaw clenched, the Styrofoam coffee cup in his hand shaking, he said his mother had once driven him into a small Missouri town and made him beg money from strangers. Two days before, she'd signed over a social-security check to a minister who had told her the Lord would provide. Later, he said, when his mother had gone back to the minister she was told that her wallet was possessed by the devil, who encouraged her spendthrift ways. The future Senator had watched his mother perform an exorcism on the kitchen table, casting the devil out of her wallet, chanting 'Satan begone.' I tend to believe this story, because of the clenched fury in his dripping face, that day, the kudzu-strangled telephone poles ticking past the back window of the steaming Lincoln, and because I have never heard him use it since.

Between fits of religiosity his mother drank; as an adult he had little patience for drinkers, which made him something of an anomaly in the Senate. At any rate, his mother died when he was fifteen and I have never heard him speak about her since that evening in Georgia.

He went to live with an aunt and uncle, attended the state university on a scholarship, married his first sweetheart, went to Harvard Law, and joined the Kennedy administration. These are the facts, the campaign bio. But try to imagine the distance between these points. Far easier to walk on your knees over broken glass from the state capital to Cambridge, Mass. and Washington DC than to do it as he did. Try to picture the days and nights devoted to work and study; you are obviously obsessed and driven to succeed or you would never have made it so far. Imagine the nights, when finally you slump over the desk, or turn off the light in the basement of your uncle's house which is your bedroom, imagine the howling demons of fear and loneliness coming in off the plains like tornadoes and rattling the windows. Imagine those few moments suspended over the abyss between work and exhausted sleep. At dawn, the exorcism would begin again.

One morning I was due to wake him up. It was New Hampshire, I think. He had a breakfast speech with the Elks or the Mooses – some antlered fraternity. I was just outside his door at the Holiday Inn when I heard the woman's voice, pleading, calling his name, and remembered her from the night before, the waitress from the cocktail lounge downstairs. Finally when she started to cry, I used my key to open the door. They were in bed. She was on her side, facing out, and he was wrapped around her. She had thrown the covers off, but she was unable to extract herself from his sleeping arms, clamped fiercely around her torso, his left hand with its wedding band clasping one of her breasts, which bulged pinkly from the cage of his clenched fingers. I finally managed to rouse him, and free her. It was to happen again, and even some of the women who managed to free themselves in the morning remarked on his tenacious reluctance, in sleep, to let go.

*   *   *

He graduated fifth in his class at Harvard Law and then signed on with Vista, the fledgling domestic version of the Peace Corps. JFK was his hero and he became acquainted with the President. I have often wondered if he knew then about JFK's satyrmania, or whether his later behavior was influenced by the eventual revelations. According to those who knew him back then, he was the straightest of arrows – like me, I like to imagine – devoted to Kennedy, to Doreen, and to the two children, avidly creating the family he'd never had.

On the anniversary of that infamous day in Dallas, I sat with him in a coffee shop in Iowa, where we had been stumping for the caucuses, and he told me that he had cried when he heard the news, sobbed uncontrollably as he hugged his secretary. Tears stood in his eyes as he told me the story. 'And then,' he said, without a trace of self-consciousness, 'I decided that I would take his place.'

He had gone back home to run for Congress, and after two terms, for the Senate. He took care of his state even as he refused to share its most conservative convictions. When he came out against the Vietnam War, early on, all agreed that his senatorial bid was ruined. His victory was seen by the national press as a signal event in the debate over the war; almost from the start, he was a national figure. He was, as unfashionable as it sounds, a hero of mine. Hero worship was especially unfashionable in the wake of the sixties, and yet I was not alone. Most of us would have worked for him for nothing. In the end, some of us did.

I grew up in the sterile, fertile state he represented, not

on one of its amber-waving farms but in an aluminum-sided suburb rimmed with shopping malls. My father sold insurance. I was a 4H captain, a stamp collector, an apple-polisher in white socks. A young nerd with aspirations to public service, I represented my state at a national high-school conference on government, flying to Washington for three days of make-believe legislative sessions and inspirational speeches from lawmakers. Castelton spoke to our group and later invited me to his office. He had a face that seemed incapable of harboring deceit or insincerity, a visage like an open door. We chatted for ten minutes. His speech about the virtues of hard work and the joys of public service might have been lifted out of a civics textbook, but I believed every word. Unlike most of the other congressmen I had met, who seemed to be speaking by rote, whose gestures and phrases sounded stagy and insincere even to a seventeen-year-old teacher's pet, he seemed absolutely sincere. Like a real person, talking man to man. What I sensed then was how much he wanted me to like him. It actually seemed to matter to him. I wanted to come to work for him then and there, but I had to wait five years. He wrote me a letter of recommendation to Harvard, and though I was accepted my father made too much to qualify for financial aid and too little to comfortably pay for Harvard so I went to the State U. A week after my graduation I was installed as an intern in his Senate office in the Dirkson building.

The years I worked with him on the Hill seem in retrospect to be the best of my life. That first year I shared a dorm-like house on the Hill near Lincoln Park with half a dozen other unpaid and underpaid press aides and interns. We walked to work, did most of our eating from canapé platters at nightly receptions and Capitol events. Later, when I became a legislative assistant, I moved to a two-bedroom apartment in Adams Morgan with Trey Davis, who also worked for the Senator. Davis was a New Yorker, one of the first of that race I had ever met. He had a year's seniority, and a world of experience, on me. He'd grown up on Fifth Avenue, attended Buckley and Hotchkiss and Williams, where he'd been the protégé of James McGregor Burns. Initially I was put off by his dangerous good looks, his arrogant and cynical manner. As my immediate superior he subjected me to a species of hazing the first few weeks and referred to me behind my back as the lemur, an allusion to my putative wide-eyed innocence. His own eyes, beneath heavy bat-wing brows, seemed knowing and cruel.

At the end of the first week he looked me up and down and said, 'You're an aesthetic menace. The polyester has got to go.' He took me to Brooks Brothers and picked out a pair of gray flannel slacks, a pair of chinos, three Oxford cloth shirts and a blue blazer which he charged to his own account. When I protested he said I could pay him back in installments. Somehow we became friends. I think I was like the plain girl who becomes the confidante of the beauty queen; he needed a protégé, an appreciative audience. When he moved to a new apartment in Adams Morgan he asked me to share. Neither of us spent much time at home, anyway. Mostly we worked. Trey would sometimes take the shuttle to New York for the weekend, returning haggard with tales of nightclubs and parties populated by dirty debutantes. He tried to explain to me the difference between downtown and uptown. I was content to stay in DC, which was more than worldly enough for me. Occasionally I would have a beer at a neighborhood pub and attempt to impress ambitious young women in Talbot's suits. Though I didn't know it at the time, it was the heyday of the pill, after Roe and before AIDS. I had a few dates and a brief, awkward romance with a Georgetown student who was interning in Senator Kennedy's office, during which I managed finally to shed my virginity at the age of twenty-three. But I wasn't very good with women. I think I was too earnest, even for the serious young ladies with Phi Beta Kappa keys and Bass weejuns who had come to the Capitol to serve their country.

When the Senator announced to the staff that he was going to make a run for the White House we were ecstatic. We would all rise with him. But more than that, we believed in him, though by then I had learned that heroes have warts. We all knew he'd had an affair with one of the assistants, whom he later placed in the office of the Senior Senator from our state. One night when I went back to the office late to retrieve some papers I saw him emerge from the inner office with a disheveled female reporter.

The Senator's face was flushed and glistening with a film of sweat. They were both giggling, until they spotted me and hurriedly donned their coats, the Senator wishing me a curt good-night.

Neat, housewifely Doreen had come to the office for the announcement. She smiled and hugged us, seeming more like the candidate's spinsterish sister than his wife. I couldn't help wondering what the campaign really meant to her. Bad enough to be the wife of a senator. But maybe he was a victim, too, married early to a woman he had outgrown. She must have looked much different to a motherless, fatherless boy at the State University than to the rising US Senator. After she left, several of us overheard Joe Tunney lecturing him from inside his office. 'Goddamnit, you've got to keep it in your pants or you're going to fuck the whole thing up,' Tunney roared. I couldn't make out the Senator's response. Tunney was a tough old Boston political operative who'd worked for Kennedy and had been with Castelton since his congressional days. Shambling red-faced out of the office, he turned to me and asked if I knew the three Bs. 'The three whats?' I asked, looking up at the broad ruined nose with its craters and exploded veins. I was afraid of him, of his caustic, whiskey breath with its whiff of decomposition and corruption. He seemed to me the antithesis of the new political order we were trying to create. 'Broads, bribes and boys,' he said. He ran his sleeve under his nose. 'Sooner or later . . .' Tunney shook his head and left the office, the sentence unfinished. I was glad to see him go. Although I might have concurred with the sentiment, it seemed out of place on this special day, this dawn of an era. I was full of liberal indignation at his crude and chauvinistic term for women, a word I'd certainly never heard on the Senator's lips.

'What about booze?' Trey Davis proposed, from the next desk over, and we all had a good laugh at Tunney's expense.

* * *

I volunteered for the campaign staff. Within days I was on the plane to Iowa with the Senator. Those first few months we were romantic underdogs, tilting at grain silos and cooling towers, drawing on a modest fund of skeptical goodwill. The Senator was a charismatic man, and if we could get five hundred people in a room, four hundred of them walked out believing. More often, it was forty. On one occasion four citizens came to hear him speak at a public library, one of them a reporter from the local weekly. But he reached out to those four as if they were convention delegates, turning his chair around backwards and sitting amongst them, lingering to chat with the blue-haired librarian who blushed and fussed with her hair as though sensing her own womanhood for the first time in a decade. And the way I looked at it, that was three more in our column. Late at night, awash in rubber-chicken indigestion and Trey's snoring from the next twin bed at the Ramadas and the Holiday Inns, I would add them up in my head like a good little accountant – the number of mouths at the church supper, the number of hands shaken outside the factory gate. And one more late convert – the receptionist who had gone off duty at eleven and joined the Senator in his room.

The Senator's close second-place finish in New Hampshire was interpreted as a win, given the large field and his last-minute gains against the polls. Suddenly money was pouring in, and the camp followers flocked. Pollsters, consultants, volunteers, fund-raisers, local politicos, party leaders, single-issue nuts, social-climbing hostesses, reporters. And women. That was when it began to get out of control.

From New Hampshire we flew straight to New York

City, where they were waiting to shower the Senator with money and attention. New York was where Carl Furst signed on. Furst was the most sought-after of Democratic political consultants, a red-faced left-wing assassin. He'd worked with the better-funded front-runner early on, but we'd been hearing that he was not happy with his candidate, and after New Hampshire, no dummy, he joined us. There were mixed feelings about this. On the one hand it was good for the team, like signing a great pitcher. But some of us, particularly Davis, who was practically running the campaign up to this point, resented this fair-weather friend, this bullet-headed mercenary. Since Furst would be stepping in at the top, everyone moved down a notch. And in fact, the Senator quickly became more and more isolated from those of us who had started out with him, cocooned in the smoky scrum of Furst and his pollsters and spin doctors.

The night before the Furst meeting we went to a party on Park Avenue given by a fat man who owned a chain of stores and his thin wife who was a former lover of Ted Kennedy. If you're wondering how I know this – they told us. That was my introduction to New York – a city I thought should be gerrymandered right out of the Republic and attached to France or maybe Turkey. At any rate, I was part of the advance team, arriving at the apartment with Trey Davis and two secret-service men. Our host and hostess greeted us at the door of their apartment, treating us with that special consideration which our association with the newly important Senator conferred. They eagerly greeted Trey by name; reminding him that their son had been at Buckley with him; Trey seemed distinctly cool at the recollection. They gave us the tour, pointing out the more prominent paintings, which were framed in gilt with little museum plaques to identify the artist. While the secret-service men harassed the kitchen staff, our host explained that he'd been a major supporter of the Democratic Party for years. 'And Evie was Ted Kennedy's lover a few years back,' he said, nodding toward his wife – who was adjusting the lilies in a large crystal vase – beaming like a man who has just commended his wife's cooking or business acumen. I thought this admission bizarre enough with his wife out of earshot, but later, arm around the tanned and beaming Evie, he repeated it to the Senator. If she had been slightly younger or prettier I'm sure he would have been very keen on this admission.

That party was the beginning of the show-biz phase. Several screen stars were on hand – apparently some of them live in New York, though I can't imagine why. The writer Norman Mailer arrived with his beautiful new red-haired wife. As with most of the couples in the room, she was much the taller. Dressed like a banker, Mailer rocked back on his heels when he listened and jabbed his finger into the Senator's chest when he talked. His wife smiled impishly. The Senator was enamored. He kidded with Mailer as if they'd known each other for years, and flirted with Mrs Mailer. It was hard to say which one he was more interested in; it was the first time I'd seen him star-stricken. Doreen was at the party, but like most political wives she had the gift for receding into the background, and after posing for photos she left early to catch the last shuttle back to be with the kids.

I stood in the corner and watched the rich people. You

knew they were rich not only because of the way they dressed but because it cost a thousand dollars a couple to shake the Senator's hand and exchange a few words. But the Senator had the gift for making that kind of encounter seem meaningful and I don't think anyone went away feeling cheated. Before he left he did his best to make sure everyone in the room loved him. And yet, listening to his remarks, for the first time since I had known him, I heard in his voice the third-person self-consciousness of a politician addressing the masses. What he said was not new – I'd heard much the same remarks a hundred times yet each time he seemed to me to be speaking his mind and his heart, directly, to individuals, no matter how large the group. This was one of his gifts, that he did not sound like a pol. Now, suddenly, he seemed insincere, as if his recent success had made him conscious of these sentiments as a winning formula. The phrase 'what the American people want . . .' was repeated a little too often for my taste.

That first night in New York after the New Hampshire primary he started the liaison with Amanda Greer that we all read about years later. Against everyone's advice, he accompanied her to a nightclub. Trey Davis and I tagged along in the secret-service car, trailing the actress's limo. Trey was furious. He explained to me that there were photographers outside these places and sometimes inside, that drugs were consumed openly on the premises; under normal circumstances it was his kind of scene, but we could kiss the nomination goodbye if anyone got a good shot of the Senator with his tongue in the actress's ear.

Trey jumped out of the car at a stoplight and ran over

to the limo, rapping on the smoked window until it finally slid down. After a heated exchange with the Senator, he finally negotiated a compromise. 'Look,' Trey said as he ran back to the car. 'You go take her in the front door of the club. I'll sneak our hero in the side door, I know the owner, and we'll meet you in the VIP room.' The Senator emerged from the limo and jogged to our car, grinning sheepishly as I passed. In a daze, I walked to the limo and climbed in.

She was curled in the corner of the seat, her legs folded up beneath her. Regarding me quizzically, she appeared ready to burst into laughter. Tiny as she was she seemed to have an enormous specific gravity; I sensed the car listing to the left like a boat beneath us. She was more real than anyone I had ever seen. Her hair was redder than I had imagined it would be, her eyes bluer than anything in nature. Despite the unexpected wrinkles around her eyes, or maybe because of them, I thought she was the most beautiful woman I'd ever seen. I imagined others, those who worshipped her from the movies, would be surprised by the wrinkles, whereas I could look beyond them. She was smoking a cigarette and when she spoke her voice was husky and low.

'Wouldn't we like to play Mrs Robinson to you,' she said. She unfolded her legs and leaned forward to pour more champagne in her glass. She seemed a little worse for wear, her words a little slurred. I wanted to protect her from herself and from all the people who wanted her. She talked to me as if I were an old friend as we glided above the rutted streets of New York. She asked me where I was from. I was astonished to learn she was born and raised on a farm not fifty miles from my home. She told me about her family, about leaving the farm at seventeen to come to the city and study acting. When we disembarked in front of the club, she took my arm as the flashbulbs began to pop. There were perhaps a hundred people waiting outside the door of the nightclub, but a path opened up for us. I heard her name repeated like a mantra. Someone asked, 'Who's the guy?' And at that moment I felt the envy of strangers and I almost believed that I deserved it. Whatever the circumstances, I had become part of her world.

I was bereft when, at the door of the VIP room, I got separated from her as the pony-tailed bouncer and the secret-service men swirled around us. Seeing her disappear into the crowd beyond the velvet rope I was furious beyond reason, as if I had been deprived of my rightful place by her side. I insisted to the bouncer that I was with her, to no avail. Forgetting the Senator entirely, I had imagined a romance between us.

I can't say what the VIP room was like, but what I saw in the bathroom and out on the dance floor gave me nightmares for days. After exploring the premises I waited sullenly outside the door into which Amanda had disappeared. Suddenly the Senator appeared, looking out into the crowd. Seeing me, he waved me in; the newly diplomatic bouncer stood aside. I glared at him indignantly. The Senator put his arm on my shoulder and said, 'I want you to take Amanda to her hotel suite and wait for me there. Don't let her out of your sight. And wait for me.' Looking around the small, smoky room, I spotted her gliding toward us, cigarette in one hand and champagne glass in the other, the eyes of the crowd tracking her, following her as if attached by wires. Even in her cups she maintained a kind of dignity, her liquidity contained in a graceful vessel. 'If it isn't my old friend Benjamin Braddock. My young friend. My new true blue baby boy.'

'Cal is going to take you home,' the Senator said.

'Home is where the hat is,' she said, 'and I don't wear hats. I don't wear hearts, either, except on my sleeve. Home is where you can't go again. It's in foreclosure.' She kissed the Senator on the cheek, then held her hand to her mouth in mock chagrin, looking around to see if the gesture had been noted. Then she took my arm and marched me out of the room, down the stairs and across the dance floor. If she had seemed tipsy she was quick and purposeful now in her stride, a practiced gait that blurred her passage and left bystanders double-taking, a just-short-of-running gait – like the rack of a Tennessee walking horse – which is unique to famous people who want to move between two points without getting dragged into contact with the spectating class. The Senator resorts to it on occasion, when rushing for planes, though usually he is a glutton for attention: hand-shaking, chats and photo ops.

She raced me out the side door around the crowd. Her driver, spotting her, jumped out to open the door as a photographer snapped her picture. Suddenly she put her arm around me and posed, laying her head on my shoulder, then kissing my neck. Two other photographers materialized and someone shouted, 'What's his name?' My vision was bleached out by the flashbulbs, and then we were in the limo, racing away.

Laughing, she said, 'I like to think about the photo

editors and gossip columnists scurrying around tomorrow while I'm still asleep, trying to figure out who you are so they can run the picture. And the funny thing is, they'll never be able to figure it out.' My exhilaration vanished as I realized what she was saying – that in her world, I didn't exist. She must have seen this, because the next moment she took my hand and said, 'I didn't mean it like that. It's just so awful if you take it too seriously, sometimes I want to drop my skirt and moon the silly bastards. But you are awfully cute.' She leaned forward and kissed me, caressing my lips with her tongue. I had never been kissed like that. When she drew away and reached for a glass, I wondered what I would tell the Senator. She poured herself another drink. I saw myself rescuing Amanda Greer from this life of liquor and limousines and nightclubs and false adulation. I would take this fallen angel back West, plant her in the rich black soil of the heartland, buy a farm and raise children. I would run for Congress and she would campaign for me. I didn't see the contradiction between this vision and the glamour which had dazzled me in the first place.

'The thing about fame,' she said, 'you think everyone will love you, that it's a way to become close to people.' She stopped and took a sip of her drink and just when I had decided she had lost the thread of her remarks she continued: 'And then when you're famous it drives a wedge between you and the rest of the world. A wall of glass.' She tapped the smoked glass of the window with her fingers. 'I don't think your Senator knows that yet.' I wanted to tell her that I understood, but she reached overhead and punched a button that flooded the rear compartment with loud music, then laid her head back on the seat and closed her eyes, nodding lightly in time to the music, her lipstick, I noted happily, smeared from our kiss.

We arrived at the hotel. She carried her drink in with her; the hotel doorman greeted her reverently. She had not spoken a word to me since our kiss. In the elevator I asked how long she was staying here. She looked at me as if she didn't understand the question. And then she said, 'I live here.'

The suite, was, to my eyes, a nest of luxury with its pale-peach floral carpet and antique furniture. It was nothing like any hotel room I had seen on the campaign. She went to the bar and poured herself another drink, half of which she spilled on the carpet, then picked up a phone and dialed. I sat down on the edge of a sofa. She was talking to someone named Gloria. I tried to imagine the course of the night, the course of my life. Should I go to her now and hang up the phone, take her in my arms? There was a knock on the door; she put her hand over the receiver and pointed to it, kissing the air between us. The Senator was waiting in the hallway with a secret-service man. Somehow I hadn't expected him this soon. I tried to think of something to say, some way of explaining what had happened in the limousine. He nodded to me, said, 'Thanks,' and walked into the room, leaving the secret-service man in the hall. Amanda waved to him, the phone crooked in her arm. He paced around nervously, picking up a porcelain vase from a side table and flipping it over to check its provenance. When he saw me standing in the door, he looked irritated. 'That'll be all, Cal,' he barked.

Emboldened by what I believed was love, frightened

but firm, I said, 'Senator, I think you should go back to the hotel.' He stared at me as if I had just offered to shoot him.

'The lady's not herself,' I said, 'and I don't think we want to risk any scandal at this point.'

He hissed, 'You little shit, how dare you – '

By now I was terrified, but I couldn't stop myself: 'I would like to remind you, sir, that you're married.'

At that moment Amanda hung up the phone. From behind, she threw her arms around the Senator, who was still glaring at me and looked as if he might charge me, like a bull, but for her restraint. Peering around his arm, she saw me and smiled. But there was no recognition in her glazed eyes and it was a crooked, intoxicated smile, the kind she would flash at a fan who managed to catch her eye. She lifted her arms and pulled the Senator's face down to her own, locking him in the same embrace that I had enjoyed earlier. I kept waiting for the kiss to end, waiting for inspiration. Finally I turned and walked out, my face burning, not wanting to be standing there when they finally broke apart. Crying with rage, I walked from the Carlyle to the Midtown Sheraton, hoping I would be mugged or challenged, then lay sleepless in my bed till dawn, feverish with jealousy and yearning.

Two days later a tabloid featured a smiling picture of the Senator entering the nightclub and another of the actress, but the two were not linked. I bought all the New York papers that morning, foolishly hoping for a printed picture of Amanda and me to lend some substance to my folly. The night marked a new level of recklessness on the part of the

Senator. And it changed me. I suddenly felt the drabness of my own existence. The hour I spent with Amanda made me yearn for something I had never known, or missed before. Not exactly beauty or sex or power, although all of these things, I realized, might be currency as negotiable as cash, exchangeable for this thing. I can only call it brilliance, like a surfeit of light. For a brief moment in my life, everything was more vivid. And in that moment, I felt a kinship with the Senator and his quest for glory. I understood how he could risk everything for a moment like the one I had shared in the limousine. I had risked quite a bit myself. I would have liked to discuss it with him, but we were never alone together again. After that night my career with the Senator was essentially finished. He didn't fire me then, but I was sent to Chicago to work with the new office there in a clearly demoted capacity.

When the Senator threw in the towel after Illinois, I had to pay my own way back to Washington from Chicago. While I was away I had been replaced on the Hill, and when I called the chief of staff he told me there were no openings for me at that time. I wasn't really surprised. I was still living in Adams Morgan with Trey, to whom I confessed most of the details of my disgrace. Though disillusioned with the Senator since the hiring of Furst, he was back at work on the Senate staff. Sometimes at night I heard the daughters of ambassadors and cabinet officers howling and moaning from his bedroom. For the first time in my life, I succeeded in picking up a girl at a bar and later, back home, she had to plead with me to be gentle, although in all of my thin amorous history no one has ever accused me of excessive enthusiasm.

Three months after the end of our campaign Trey came home in a rage. After paying Furst and his people, a total of more than two hundred thousand, the campaign committee declared bankruptcy. Like most of the staff, including Trey, I was owed four months in back wages. 'Can you believe that bastard?' Trey said. That night we went out to eat in an Ethiopian restaurant and Trey told me the Senator had flown up to New York twice in the last month to visit Amanda Greer. By this time I was working for a public relations firm. It was nothing I would have envisioned myself doing five months before and I was not always proud of the work. Among others we represented a South American dictator who for years had been the target of criticism from the Senator for his appalling human rights record. I was, however, having more success with women. After my moment of glory with Amanda Greer, I felt slightly disdainful of mortal females, which seemed to make me more attractive. For six months I dated a legislative assistant from Texas named Deirdre Clark who would have married me, who I probably would have been thrilled to marry a year before. She was coltish and sweet and smarter than me. I cheated on her and let her find out and she moved back to Houston a few months later.

Trey had increasing difficulties with Castleton and eventually went to work for Senator Moynihan. Three years after our campaign ended Castelton officially announced he was making another run. Now he was the front runner. According to Trey, fat-faced Carl Furst had agreed to run the campaign only after the Senator promised to stop fucking around. A week after he won New Hampshire, one of the supermarket tabloids published a story about the Senator's relationship with Amanda Greer. Lacking hard evidence, they published a picture of the two tête-à-tête at a fundraiser. Unnamed sources said that the Senator made frequent, unscheduled visits to New York and that his wife had given him an ultimatum. The issue of the Senator's womanizing, which had been the secret buzz of the press corps for years, was now out in the open. At a press conference in Florida the Senator was pelted with questions about the relationship and about his fidelity. He indignantly denied the story, while acknowledging 'an old friendship' with the actress. With Doreen standing at his side, he said, 'I have always been a faithful husband and a devoted father,' and refused to say more. He accused the press of conducting a witch hunt and suggested that the story was the work of his rivals and of the Republicans. The issue bubbled for a week and then faded with the lack of new disclosures.

A few days after the Senator's Super Tuesday victories, Trey organized a reunion poker game for some of us who had been involved in the previous campaign. We met at a saloon in Georgetown. Trey had reserved a private room in the back. He asked us all to bring two hundred dollars for the game. The party consisted of Gene Samuels, Dave Crushak, Tom Whittle, myself and Trey. We drank beer and reminisced about the bad old days on the trail. All of us had been burned when the previous committee had declared bankruptcy. None of us was involved with the new one. If the American public were listening in, they would not have formed a favorable impression of Castleton's character. Old slights and grievances were revived, along with tawdry stories of the Senator's broom-closet dalliances. We reviewed the specifications of 'the type,' blonde, big tits, no ass. Finally, Dave Crushak said, 'I'm feeling lucky. Who's got the cards?'

'I've got a card,' said Trey. From his blazer he extracted a five-by-seven picture of an attractive blonde on which was printed the name Tamara along with a set of measurements and the name and number of a Los Angeles modelling agency. We passed the card around, making appreciative noises. We were all a little drunk by now. 'Look familiar?' Trey asked. When no one could place her, he said, 'The type, boys. The fucking archetype.' It was true. She looked like a composite of all the stewardesses and receptionists and students. Leaning forward and leering beneath the arched bat-wings of his eyebrows, Trey explained: 'The game, gentlemen, is one-card stud, no draw, two-hundred-dollar ante.' I had dim suspicions of the nature of the game, but I thought he must be kidding. We all fell silent. Trey looked smug. He had our attention.

'I met Tamara in New York, where she began her modelling career. Not only is Tamara a model, she's also, surprise surprise, an actress. An aspiring actress. But it's not easy to break into the business. Lot of competition. Lot of pretty faces. Ditto for modelling. Tamara has to pay her rent. And she likes a good time. So she mixes some business with her pleasure, what the hell, you like a guy, you let him buy you dinner. Or a gram of coke. Why not let him pay your rent? Quid pro quo. Semi pro.'

'I'm a happily married man,' Gene Samuels said nervously, misreading the intro.

'Ignorance is bliss, Gene. As usual you are way behind us. Now let's say you're a young aspiring actress like

Tamara. Wouldn't you kill to get invited to the house of a major studio head? And even better, what if it gave you a chance to meet a handsome young senator?'

'If you're saying what I think you're saying . . .' said Dave Crushak, who didn't finish his sentence.

Trey explained that the Senator would be attending a fundraiser at the home of a studio boss in LA next week. A college buddy of his who owed him a favor would be attending. He proposed to send Tamara along as the friend's date and let nature – the Senator's nature – take its course. Under skeptical questioning from the rest of us he explained that Tamara would actively solicit and encourage the Senator's attentions. To that end we would pay her a thousand dollars. Another college buddy, a reporter at the *LA Times*, would be happy to watch Tamara's apartment in Santa Monica that night, on the offchance that anything newsworthy took place. We all raised a dozen practical objections, somehow unwilling to voice the moral ones. Like the Senator, Trey was a magnetic individual. The rest of us envied and feared him. If one of us had raised his voice in indignation the others would surely have followed, but no one wanted to seem priggish. And all of us felt betrayed. I think in the end I told myself the scheme was unlikely to succeed and thus absolved myself as I put my two hundred dollars on the table.

And that, basically, was how it happened, though I have had to change some of the details for obvious reasons. This was years ago, but I haven't been able to forget. Tamara was famous for a minute and a half, landing a role in a TV pilot which never aired. Trey married one of his debutantes, the daughter of a liberal philanthropist. Amanda Greer, whose screen career as a femme fatale had been fading for some time, did a well-publicized stint at the Betty Ford Clinic and was subsequently cast as the star of a TV series which is still running. I saw her two years ago in the Jockey Club at the Ritz Carlton, where I was dining with a client and she was being feted by a large party. I'd read in the *Post* that she was in town to film an episode. She spotted me as she came in and I guessed from her puzzled expression that she half-remembered me. Several times during dinner I saw her squinting over, trying to place me. When she excused herself from the table, I followed. She was standing in front of the phone booth, waiting for me. 'Do I know you?' she demanded.

'I worked for the Senator,' I said, looking down, unable to hold her gaze. She was still beautiful and if anything looked younger.

'Ah yes,' she said finally. 'Benjamin Braddock.'

I nodded.

'You know the crazy thing?' she said. 'He hardly touched me. Mainly he just wanted to hold and be held. That was all. He'd fall asleep with his arms around me and hang on for dear life.' She looked very sad, although I had grown old enough to wonder if it was genuine sadness or the mask of an actress. 'I felt so bad for him.' She searched my face for a moment, her expression almost imploring, and I wanted to say something but suddenly I didn't trust my voice. She sighed and nodded, then turned away and disappeared into the ladies' room. When she finally returned to her table I was unable to catch her eye.

The former Senator has an active consulting business,

and as the scandal fades in the public memory he is more often called upon to comment on world and national events. He is writing his memoirs. Doreen stood by him and by all accounts their marriage has actually flourished. I am not so cynical as to claim any credit for this, or to suggest that it was part of the plan or that it absolves me in any way. The republic is on its knees, governed by men without character or conviction. I don't know that Castelton could have won, or that having won he would have preserved any of the ideals of the man whom I had first gone to work for, fresh from my American history seminars. At the age of thirty-three I have lost or betrayed most of my own ideals. Having had so direct a hand in ruining him, I blame myself, as I am sure he blames himself, but I'm pretty disgusted with the rest of you, too.

Another election is upon us, and Trey is running for Congress from Manhattan, bankrolled by his father-in-law. They say he's settled down and that he's faithful to his wife. He's expected to win handily, and I'm confident that he will.

THE BUSINESS

I'D HEARD ALL THE jokes before I moved out here. But still, you think Hollywood will be different for you. You say to yourself, Sure it's a jungle, but I'm Dr Livingstone.

I graduated from Columbia with a degree in English lit and went to work for a newspaper in Bergen County, just across the river from Manhattan, keeping my cheap apartment on West 111th Street where I lived with my girlfriend. My thesis was a poststructuralist analysis of film adaptations of major American novels, and within a year I'd wangled the job of movie reviewer and entertainment reporter. I loved the movies, always have. The idea of being a screenwriter came to me during a group interview with a writer/director who was in Manhattan flacking for his new picture. It wasn't the fact that he didn't seem particularly bright, or that he made his ascent sound so haphazard and effortless, but something more visceral – the way he looked sitting there smoking a cigarette with the light coming through the window of the fortieth-floor corporate tower. I could see the pores in his skin and the stubble of his beard, and there was something green stuck between two of his teeth.

And I suddenly thought, That could be me sitting there with two days' growth and a green thing on my teeth.

I didn't quit my job that day or anything, but I did start writing screenplays, renting films I loved and studying their structure, thinking about what they had in common. I was abetted in this by my aunt Alexis, who once had been a contract player at Paramount. She'd been in a couple of westerns with John Wayne and was briefly married to a director. After the divorce she moved to New York; the director had made her quit the movies, she said, and it was too late to go back, but she still talked as if she were a member of a warm extended family called 'the business.' She claimed as friends some relatively famous folks, and she read *Variety* and the *Hollywood Reporter* faithfully. I knew from our actual family that she'd been somewhat badly used out there, but she wasn't bitter. Now she gave acting lessons and occasionally did community theater. When I moved to New York, she more or less adopted me. My parents were divorced, fading into the orange sunsets of Arizona and Florida, respectively.

Alexis lived in faded elegance in a grand prewar building over near Sutton Place, a duplex she'd occupied for years, the first couple with her third husband, and which she couldn't have afforded if not for rent control. Even with a severely depressed rent she'd had to sublet the more luxurious lower floor, which was separated by two doors from her own quarters upstairs. The centerpiece of the downstairs apartment was a spectacular canopy bed replete with rose-colored chintz drapery. Alexis herself slept in the upstairs parlor on a pullout sofa. The lower floor was occupied by the manager of a rock group who was burning holes in all the upholstery. Alexis knew because she snuck down and snooped around whenever he wasn't home.

Alexis encouraged my screenwriting ambitions and read my earliest attempts. She also provided the only good advice I've ever gotten on the subject. 'Dalton Trumbo once told me the secret of a screenplay,' she said, mixing herself a negroni in the closet which served her as kitchen, pantry and bar. At six in the evening the fading light was slicing through the mullioned windows at a forty-five-degree angle – that second-to-last light thick and yellow with doomed bravado – and making the dust swimming through the apartment seem like movie mist. 'He was a lovely man, much misunderstood. That McCarthy stuff – terrible. But as I was starting to say, Dalton said to me one night – I think we were at the Selznicks', and I said, "Dalton, what's your secret?" and he whispered something in my ear which I won't repeat. I gave him a little slap on the wrist, not that I really minded. I was flattered and told him so, but I was still married to the fag – before I found out, of course. So I said to Dalton, "No, no, what's the secret of a great *screenplay*?" And he said, "It's very simple, Lex. Three acts: first act, get man up tree; second act, shake a stick at him; third act, get him down."'

When she was really in her cups Alexis told me she'd call Swifty Lazar or some other great friend of hers and fix me up, the exquisitely carved syllables of her trained speech softening, liquefying like the cubes in her glass. But the fact is she didn't have any juice in the industry. I didn't mind. I eventually landed an agent on my own, at which point I figured it was time to make the leap of faith. Plus my girlfriend announced that she was in love with my best friend and that they'd been sleeping together for six months.

I sublet my apartment and rented a place in Venice three blocks from the beach. This was in February, and I loved exchanging the frozen, rotten city for a place smelling of flowers and the ocean. At the same time, more than anywhere else in Southern California, Venice reminded me of New York with its general shabbiness. There were plenty of bums, just so I wouldn't get too homesick, and the crime rate was also pretty impressive. But basically I felt the same way about California that Keats did about Chapman's Homer. I quit smoking, ate plenty of fruit and vegetables, started sleeping regular hours.

One thing I didn't do was rush out to join AA, which was just then becoming really hip. If I had, I probably would've met some girls. But I was still under the thrall of the writer-as-holy-lush idea. Who could imagine Raymond Chandler sober? One of my favorite stories involved Herman Mankiewicz, the other genius behind *Citizen Kane*, who arrived drunk one night – not uncharacteristically – at an elaborate A-list dinner party. He then got drunker, and finally evacuated the contents of his stomach all over the table. As the other guests looked on horrified, Mankiewicz turned to his hostess and said, 'Don't worry – the white wine came up with the fish.'

In Venice, my second-story studio had a little terrace off the back. I'd wake up early most mornings and take my computer out there, overlooking a tiny courtyard choked with cacti, palms and flowering bushes. Having grown up in the intemperate zones, I'm still a little thrilled by the sight of a palm tree. My landlady believed that nature should be allowed to take its course and just let it all grow. The couple across the way believed in nature too; they fucked at all hours with the shades up and I couldn't help seeing them, usually her bobbing up and down on top of him, facing me. I guess she was performing. Maybe she thought I was a casting director . . . Anyway, I appreciated it, since that was as close as I was getting to carnal knowledge.

My second screenplay opens with this very scene, close on couple making love, girl on top, camera pulling back out the window, pulling back, reverse angle on the guy watching from his terrace. Eventually the girl and the guy on the terrace – a writer, of course – meet and have this incredible affair. She decides to leave her boyfriend, but of course he turns out to be a coke dealer involved with some very heavy Colombians, and the girl knows enough about the gang to implicate them in a murder. Except she doesn't realize it until . . .

Believe it or not, this screenplay attracted the interest of a fairly important producer. That was when I first met Danny Brode. The producer had a first-look deal with the studio where Brode was the new vice-president of production. The meeting Brode scheduled for me was my first with a studio executive. I spent about three hours that morning trying to figure out what to wear and whether to shave. Finally I shaved and put on a white shirt, tie, blazer and jeans. Brode made me wait an hour, and when I was ushered into his dazzling white office he shook my hand and said, 'What, you got a funeral or a wedding today?' When I looked baffled he said, 'The tie, dude.' So I knew

I'd worn the wrong thing, and knew he knew I'd worn the tie for him.

Brode was wearing jeans and a work shirt which barely held him in. Standing about five foot six, the man weighed three hundred if he weighed an ounce. He had D cup cheeks, and his chin would've made another man's potbelly. Not exactly the guy to be handing out advice on appearances. Anyway, he told me he'd been running late all day and had to drive out to the Valley to check on a film in postproduction, could we take the meeting in his car?

We went out to the parking lot and got in his car, which was this four-door Maserati sedan. I didn't even know Maserati made sedans, but figured Brode was too big to drive around in one of the sports models. On the drive out to the Valley he spent most of the time on his car phone, but in between he listened as I pitched like crazy. Finally he said, 'Instead of a writer, how about if this guy's an artist. We move the thing from Venice to San Francisco, and he's got a humongous studio filled with canvases – and right out the window he sees the couple screwing. The art thing's very hot right now and this way we'll get a lot more visuals.' I don't know, I probably would've made him into a female impersonator. I was dying to get into the game, my savings were exhausted, my Subaru needed new brakes, and I had yet to meet a girl who wanted to go out to dinner with an unemployed screenwriter. My ex-best friend had just written to say he and my ex-girlfriend were getting married, and he hoped I didn't have any hard feelings. After pretending to think deeply about Brode's suggestion for a minute, I said, 'I like it. I think I could make it work.'

He dropped me at the gate of the soundstage and gave me a business card from a car service. 'We'll work it out with your agent.' I stood around baking in the sun for an hour before the car finally came to take me back to the studio. That night I bought a bottle of Spanish bubbly, which I knocked back on the terrace while my neighbors traded orgasms.

I called Alexis in New York, and she told me that I was part of the big family. We talked for an hour, and for once I believe I matched her drink for drink. Then I thought about calling my old girlfriend, imagining her chagrin when she realized what she'd given up, but passed out instead.

'Martin, darling, I'm going to make you a rich man,' my agent told me a week later. She'd grown up on Long Island and had only been out here a couple years, but she talked just like something out of *What Makes Sammy Run*. They must give you a copy at LAX or something, I don't know why I never got mine.

The deal was two drafts plus revisions at scale, which if not a great deal was more money than I made in a year at the newspaper. And I was thrilled to have a foot in the door. 'Danny Brode's really big,' my agent said without a trace of irony. 'That man is going places, and he can take you with him.'

'I don't feel like going to the fat farm,' I said.

'You better start watching your mouth around this town,' my agent said. 'It's a small community, and if you want to be part of it, you've got to play by the rules. Bo Goldman and Bob Towne can afford to be smartasses, but you can't.'

'Could you send me a list of these rules?' I was so happy

I couldn't help being full of myself. The next week she took me to lunch at Spago and introduced me to several people she described as important players, calling me 'Martin Brooks, the writer.'

Then I started writing the draft that would transform my hero into a painter. I flew up to San Francisco for atmosphere, talked to gallery owners and artists. Just dropping the studio's name opened doors, and I implied that a major star was interested in the lead. Back home I was able to get an interview with an LAPD narcotics detective who filled me in on the inner workings of the drug cartels.

Ten weeks after the papers were signed, I handed in my new draft. The next day I got a FedEx package with Danny Brode's card attached to a bottle of Cristal. Only his name – no title, studio, address or phone number – was printed on the card. *Danny Brode*. No need to wear a tie around here. Anyway, drinking that bottle of Cristal was the high point of the whole experience.

The hangover set in a couple weeks later when my agent called. 'Basically they're thrilled with the script. Ecstatic. But they want to talk to you about a couple of little changes.'

'No problem,' I said. 'We're contracted for two drafts, right? I mean, I make another ten grand or so for a rewrite.'

'Don't worry your genius brain about it. Just take the meeting and we'll see what they want.'

What they wanted was a completely different story. Having fallen in love with his idea of the art world back-drop, Brode now wanted a movie about how commerce corrupts artists. Columbia had an art project in development, and he was determined to beat its release. We could keep the drug element – the big-shot gallery owner was also involved in the coke trade. I sat in Brode's huge white office, trying to figure out where the white walls ended and the white-leather furniture began, trying to see the virtues of this new story and to recognize some shred of my own script.

Nodding like an idiot, I practically called him a genius and said I didn't know why I hadn't seen all this potential in the first place. Back home, though, I called my agent and screamed at her about the stupidity of studio executives and the way art was corrupted by commerce. She listened patiently. Finally I concluded, 'Well, at least I get paid to be a whore.'

She said, 'Try and pick out the virtues in his concept. I'll work on the money.'

'What do you mean, "work on the money"? It's in the contract.'

'Of course,' she said.

I sat down again and tried to be professional about the whole thing, which is to say I tried not to give a shit. Three weeks later I delivered the new draft. I'd just bought a new car, a little Beamer, with my first check. When my agent called one morning to talk about another project, I said, 'When do I get paid for my second draft?'

'We're calling that a polish instead of a draft.'

'A *polish*? It was a *whole new story*, however stupid. I knocked myself out. Are you trying to tell me I'm not getting paid? What about the contract?'

'Look, Martin, you're new at this. Brode says it's a polish, and he wants you to do one more polish before he shows it to the head of production.'

I was beginning to understand. 'You mean I get paid for a second draft, but it's not a draft unless Brode says it is.'

'Let's just say it behooves us to give Danny Brode some slack at this point. You don't want to get known as a difficult writer. Give him one more polish and I promise you it'll be worth your while in the long run.'

When I threatened to go to the Writers Guild, she said she'd hate to end our professional relationship.

Maybe you've heard the one about the devil who goes to the agent and says, 'I'll give you any client you want – Cruise, Costner, Pacino, you name it, in exchange for your immortal soul for all eternity.' And the agent says, 'What's the catch?'

I stopped trusting my agent from that moment on, but I followed her advice. I wrote three drafts, got paid for one, and the project was in turnaround within six months. Though I didn't see Brode for a couple of years, in a sense my agent was right. I was bankable because I'd had a deal, and that led to other deals, and within a couple years I had my first movie in production and moved into a house in Benedict Canyon. And whenever I needed a villain for a story, someone rich and powerful to harass the protagonists, I had vivid impressions to draw on.

Danny Brode became even more rich and powerful. He married into a Hollywood dynasty and shortly thereafter was running the studio his in-laws controlled. Consolidation of power through marriage was established procedure in this particular family. Brode's father-in-law was supposed to be affiliated with a major crime family. In the film community it was whispered that in a premarital conference Brode had been made to understand cheating on his wife would constitute his precipitous fall from grace. This was considered slightly bizarre, since everybody fucked around in proportion to their power and wealth, most of all people who owned studios and casinos. But the old boy was apparently overfond of his first daughter.

'Some nice Faustian elements in this situation,' I said to the lunch partner who first filled me in on this story. I once heard someone say there are only seven basic stories, but in this business there's only one. In Hollywood the story is always Faust.

'Some nice what?' he said.

I smiled. 'I was just thinking of an old German film.'

Brode got even fatter. In a town where everybody had a personal trainer and green salads were considered a main course, there was something almost heroic about his obesity. From time to time I would see him at Morton's or wherever, and after a while – once CAA took over my representation, for example, and I started dating actresses – he even began to recognize me. I heard stories. My first agent was right – the bitch. It's a small town.

One of the stories I heard was about a novelist I knew from Columbia. After his first novel made him famous he star-tripped out here to soak up some of the gravy. Success came on him pretty fast, and he ran so fast to keep up with it that he got out in front of it. He bought a million-dollar co-op on Central Park West and a beach house in Maine plus he had a little problem with the C word. He'd sold his book to Brode's studio outright, which is to say he got paid the same no matter whether it went into production or not. By the time the second payment was due, this writer was pretty desperate for money – he was overdue on both his mortgages, his girlfriend had an insatiable wardrobe, and his wife was socking him for a big settlement. Brode knew about this. So when it came time to pay off, he called the writer up to his house in Malibu and he said, 'Look, I owe you a quarter mil, but at this point I don't know if we're going to go into production. Things are tight and your sex appeal is fading. Let's just say either I could give you seventy-five and we could call it even. Or I could tie you up in court for the next ten years.' The writer starts screaming about the contract, his agency, the Writers Guild. And Brode says, 'Talk to your agent. I think he'll see it my way.'

Even in Hollywood this is not standard procedure, but the writer's stock had dropped; after being hot for a season, he'd cooled off fast, and the agency, after a lot of thought, decided to go with Brode and advised the writer to take the seventy-five and shut up.

By the time I heard this story I wasn't even surprised. I'd learned a lot in three years.

I was doing well by local standards, and that I found myself doing business with Brode again wasn't really surprising. Several production companies were tracking an idea of mine when Brode told my agency he wanted to work with me. CAA packaged a deal with me, a director and two stars for a story about – well, let's just say it was a story of betrayal and revenge. This was the one I'd been wanting to do from the beginning. 'A Yuppie *Postman Always Rings Twice*' was the one-liner devised by my agent. For a variety of reasons, some of them aesthetic, it was important to me that the movie be shot in New York. Brode wanted to do it in Toronto and send a second unit to New York for a day. Toronto was far cheaper, and thought to resemble Manhattan. I knew I couldn't change any producer's mind when two or three million dollars were at stake, so I worked on the director. He was a man with several commercially successful films behind him who was dying to be an auteur. He couldn't understand how the kind of respect that Scorsese and Coppola got had thus far eluded him, so it wasn't hard to convince him that New York's critical fraternity would take his film much more seriously if it was *authentic*; that is to say, if it was shot in New York. You couldn't fake these things, I said, not even in the movies. You think Woody Allen would shoot a movie in Toronto, or that they'd publish him in *The New Yorker* if he did? Or consider Sidney Lumet, I reminded him.

That did it. Though Brode kicked and screamed, the director was adamant and very eloquent; besides, his clout far exceeded mine, commercially. In the end, after I'd handed in the third draft, they headed off to New York with long lines of credit and suitcases full of cash for the friendly local Teamsters, who for all I knew were distantly related to Danny Brode.

I went along for preproduction, since the director'd decided he liked having me around; so long as I didn't ask for a consulting fee, the studio was happy to pay my expenses. Brode's assistant, a woman named Karen

Levine, would be on location, while he would fly out once in a while to check in. Levine was so petite, blonde and terribly efficient that at first I hardly noticed her. In Los Angeles one can become accustomed to thinking of beauty as something languid, sexiness as a quality that adheres only to the slow-moving, self-conscious forms of actresses and professional companions. And while Karen was no odalisque, I began noticing her more and more. Despite the legendary informality of Southern California – the indiscriminate use of first names, the gross overextension of the concept of friendship – it was unusual to encounter someone who could sail straight between the whirlpool of craven servility and the shoals of condescension. Karen did, and I liked her for it. That she was doing more than working for Brode had occurred to me, but my discreet inquiries suggested they were strictly business and that Brode was living up to the contract with his father-in-law.

Then I heard Karen say she was looking to rent an apartment for the three months of filming. I thought of Alexis, who had finally thrown the rock manager out, losing several thousand in the process. I figured the studio would pay a rent bloated enough to make up some of what Hollywood had taken out of her in the old days. Alexis would be thrilled by her renewed proximity to 'the business', and I liked the idea of doing Karen a favor.

We were both staying at the Sherry-Netherland, and one afternoon I walked her over to Sutton Place. She'd grown up in Pasadena and was a little nervous about Manhattan, so I wanted her to see the city at its best. On a cool day at the end of April, the air was crisp and swept clean by a light breeze. Across the street the Plaza glowed white in the sun.

The daffodils on Park Avenue were blooming in the center median, and the doormen stood guard at the entrances of the grand old buildings. Karen looked casually tremendous in an Irish sweater and jeans; I felt like a boy returning to his own country after making good in the colonies.

Alexis greeted us in a flowing caftan, kissed Karen on both cheeks and ushered us into the upstairs parlor where she'd laid out a tea service that would've done Claridges proud. She then took us on a tour, pointing out pictures of herself with the Duke, and Bogie, a signed first edition from Faulkner, a set of candlesticks given to her by Red Skelton, the love seat on which she'd traded confidences (here she winked) with Errol Flynn. Some of this stuff even I hadn't heard before. She was laying it on a bit thick, but Karen seemed both attentive and relaxed. When we went downstairs I knew Karen was hooked as soon as she saw the big canopy bed floating in the middle of the big paneled bedroom, wreathed in rose-colored chintz. Before Alexis had mixed her second negroni – 'I don't usually drink in the afternoon, but this is an occasion, are you sure you won't have one?' – it was decided that Karen would move in for the three months and that Alexis would introduce her to the landlord as her niece; the rock manager had been her 'nephew.'

When we finally left at six, I asked Karen out to dinner. She said she had a lot of work to do but would love to some other night.

When shooting started, I hung around and visited the set every couple days. Brode flew in most weekends, which surprised me, though he seemed to be taking an excessive interest in the project. Each of his visits managed to make someone miserable. Three weeks into shooting it was me. Having decided he didn't like the ending, he wanted an upbeat rewrite. I kicked and screamed about the integrity of the story. Then I tried to go through the director; but Brode had worked on him first, and he was impervious to my warnings about what *The New Yorker* would think of the new ending. Apparently he was more concerned about his two points of the gross.

'It comes down to this, Martin,' Brode said as he sawed into a veal chop one night at Elaine's. 'You write the new ending or we hire somebody else. I'll give you another twenty-five, call it consulting.' I watched him insert half a pound of calf's flesh into his maw, waiting for him to choke on it and die. It occurred to me that he was too fat for anybody to successfully perform the Heimlich maneuver, so I could say to the police officers, *Hey, sorry, I tried to get my arms around him, but no go*.

I rewrote the ending. For me it ruined the movie, but the American public bought sixty million dollars' worth of tickets, a big gross at the time.

I visited Alexis frequently and used these occasions to knock on Karen's door. One night she finally allowed me to take her to dinner. I told her what I'd never told anyone before, about how my ex-New York girlfriend ran off and married my best friend. Karen was appalled and sympathetic. By now she'd adopted the Manhattan uniform of nighttime femininity, looking very sexy in a small, tight black dress. At her door we exchanged an encouraging kiss, but when it began to develop into something else she pulled back and announced she had to be up at five.

A week or so later I went over to visit Alexis. As she was mixing the negronis she said, 'Who's Karen's boyfriend, anyway? I take it he's some big shot.'

'I don't think she has a boyfriend,' I said, somewhat alarmed.

'I can't understand how someone as pretty as Karen could let that fat man touch her.'

I felt relieved. 'That wasn't Karen's boyfriend, it was her boss.'

Alexis snorted. 'Call it what you want. I know all about girls and their bosses.'

'It's not like that with Karen.'

'Don't tell me what it's like,' she said. 'I have to listen to them. And now I have to buy a new bed.'

'What're you talking about?'

She put a finger to her lips, walked over to open the stairway door and listened. Then she motioned for me to follow her down.

The canopy bed was wrecked. The box spring and mattress which had previously floated a couple feet off the floor were now earthbound, the bedposts and chintz draperies tangled and splayed.

'I've had bosses like that,' Alexis said. 'But thank God I never had that one. The poor girl's risking her life every time she climbs into bed with that whale.'

Brode had flown back to the West Coast that morning, so I had a whole week to plot my strategy. I called a meeting as soon as he got back to town. The only time he could meet me was breakfast: the Regency, at seven-thirty.

When I arrived at eight he was just finishing off a plate

of ham and eggs. 'I'm just leaving,' he said. 'What's up?'

'I have another movie. You might like this one.'

'What's the pitch?' he said. 'I've got exactly three minutes.'

'It's a mob story.'

'That turf's pretty well worked,' he said.

'You'll like this one,' I said. In my story, a young mobster's career takes off when he marries the don's daughter. But there's a catch: if he ever screws around, the don tells him, he'll be a piss-poor scuba diver, fifty feet under without oxygen. At first the son-in-law does very well. However, a young wise guy within the organization happens to live in the same building as this very attractive girl, and there's a farcical scene involving this broken bed. The broken bed leads to very dire consequences for some of the parties concerned.'

Brode's face turned dark red as he listened. At the end of the pitch he looked into my eyes to see if he might've misheard me. Then he said, 'What do you want?'

'I want another movie with you. Okay, maybe not this one, but something else. And I want to coproduce.'

'I could have you . . .' He didn't finish.

And that's how I became a producer, on terms that were highly satisfactory from my point of view. I don't think Danny felt it was the best deal he'd ever made, and I knew I'd have to watch out for him. But the project I eventually developed made money for both of us, which made me feel a little safer when falling asleep at night.

A year after this breakfast I flew back to New York for Alexis's funeral. One of ten mourners, I cried when they lowered her coffin into the ground out in the cemetery in Queens. The last time I remembered crying was on a day that should've been one of my happiest. I'd just gotten a call from an agent in Los Angeles who'd read my script and decided to represent me. I waited two hours for Lauren, my girlfriend, to come home from work. I bought flowers and champagne and called everyone I knew. Finally Lauren got home and I almost knocked her over. We'd talked about moving to California together if anything happened for me. I poured champagne and talked about our future in the promised land. 'We can live near the beach,' I said, following her into the bathroom, where she rubbed a pink towel back and forth across her dark hair. 'We'll drive up to Big Sur on weekends.' That was when she told me. One minute I've got champagne streaming down my face, and tears the next. I thought about that as I listened to the words of the minister at the cemetery, and felt the wetness on my cheeks. I remembered that day years ago in a one-bedroom apartment on West 111th Street as being the last time I cried. I don't think it will happen again.

CON DOCTOR

THEY'VE COME FOR YOU *at last. Outside your cell door, gathered like a storm. Each man holds a pendant sock and in the sock is a heavy steel combination lock which he has removed from the locker in his own cell. You feel them out there, every predatory one of them, and still they wait. They have found you. Finally they crowd open the cell door and pour in, flailing at you like mad drummers on amphetamines, their cats' eyes glowing yellow in the dark, hammering at the recalcitrant bones of your face and the tender regions of your prone carcass, the soft tattoo of blows interwoven with grunts of exertion. It's the old lock 'n' sock. You should have known. As you wait for the end, you think that it could've been worse. It has been worse. Christ, what they do to you some nights . . .*

In the morning, over seven-grain cereal and skim milk, Terri says, 'The grass looks sick.'

'You want the lawn doctor,' McClarty says. 'I'm the con doctor.'

'I wish you'd go back to private practice. I can't believe you didn't report that inmate who threatened to kill you.'

McClarty now feels guilty that he told Terri about this little incident – a con named Lesko who made the threat after McClarty cut back his Valium – in the spirit of stoking her sexual ardor. His mention of the threat, his exploitation of it, have the unintended effect of making it seem more real.

'The association is supposed to take care of the grass,' McClarty says. They live in a community called Live Oakes Manor, two-to-four-bedroom homes behind an eight-foot brick wall, with four tennis courts, a small clubhouse and a duck pond. This is the way we live now – on culs-de-sac in false communities. Bradford Arms, Ridgeview Farms, Tudor Crescent, Wedgewood Heights, Oakdale Manor, Olde Towne Estates – these capricious appellations with their diminutive suggestion of the baronial, their faux Anglo-pastoral allusiveness. Terri's two-bedroom unit with sundeck and Jacuzzi is described in the literature as 'contemporary Georgian.'

McClarty thinks about how, back in the days of pills and needles – of Percodan and Dilaudid and finally fentanyl – he didn't have these damn nightmares. In fact he didn't have any dreams. Now when he's not dreaming about the prison, he dreams about the pills and also about the powders and the deliquescent Demerol mingling in the barrel of the syringe with his own brilliant blood. He dreams that he can see it glowing green beneath the skin like a radioactive isotope as it moves up the vein, warming everything in its path until it blossoms in his brain stem. Maybe, he thinks, he should go to a meeting.

'I'm going to call this morning,' Terri continues. 'And have them check the gutters while they're at it.' She will, too. Her remarkable sense of economy and organization, which might seem comical or even obnoxious, is touching to McClarty, who sees it as a function of her recovering alcoholic's battle against chaos. He admires this. And he likes the fact that she knows how to get the oil in the cars changed or free upgrades when they fly to St Thomas. Outside of the examining room McClarty still feels bereft of competence and will.

She kisses his widow's peak on her way out and reminds him about dinner with the Clausens, whoever they might be. God bless them and their tchotchkes. Perversely, McClarty actually likes this instant new life. Just subtract narcotics and vodka, and stir. He feels like a character actor who, given a cameo in a sitcom, finds himself written into the series as a regular. He moved to this southeastern city less than a year ago, after graduating from rehab in Atlanta, and lived in an apartment without furniture until he moved in with Terri.

McClarty met her at a Mexican restaurant and was charmed by her air of independence and unshakable self-assurance. She leaned across the bar and said, 'Fresh jalapeños are a lot better. They have them, but you have to ask.' She waved her peach-colored nails at the bartender. 'Carlos, bring the gentleman some fresh peppers.' Then she turned back to her conversation with a girlfriend, her mission apparently complete.

A few minutes later, sipping his Perrier, McClarty couldn't help overhearing her say to her girlfriend, 'Ask *before* you go down on him, silly. Not after.'

McClarty admires Terri's ruthless efficiency. Basically she has it all wired. She owns a clothing store, drives an Acura, has breasts shaped like mangoes around an implanted core of saline. *Not* silicone, she announced virtuously, the first night he touched them. If asked she can review the merits of the top plastic surgeons in town. 'Dr Milton's really lost it,' she'll say. 'Since he started fucking his secretary and going to Aspen his brow lifts are getting scary. He cuts way too much and makes everybody look either frightened or surprised.' At forty, with his own history of psychological reconstruction, McClarty doesn't hold a few nips and tucks against a girl. Particularly when the results are so exceptionally pleasing to the eye.

'You're a *doctor*?' Instead of saying, *Yes, but just barely*, he nodded. Perched as she was on a stool that first night, her breasts seemed to rise on the swell of this information. Checking her out when he first sat down, Dr Kevin McClarty thought she looked like someone who would be dating a pro athlete, or a guy with a new Ferrari who owned a chain of fitness centers. She is almost certainly a little too brassy and provocative to be the consort of a doctor, which is one of the things that excites Kevin about her; making love to her, he feels simultaneously that he is slumming and sleeping above his economic station. Best of all, she is in the program, too. When he heard her order a virgin margarita he decided to go for it. A week after the jalapeños, he moved in with her.

The uniformed guard says, 'Good morning Dr McClarty,' as he drives out the gate on his way to work. Even after all these years he gets a kick out of hearing the honorific attached to his own name. He grew up even more in awe of doctors than most mortals because his mother, a nurse, told him that his father was one, though she refused all further entreaties for information. Raised in the bottom half of a narrow, chilly two-flat in Evanston, Illinois, he still doesn't quite believe in the reality of this new life – the sunshine, the walled and gated community, the smiling guard who calls him Doctor. Perversely, he believes in the dream, which is far more realistic than all this blue sky and imperturbable siding. He doesn't tell Terri, though. He never tells her about the dreams.

Driving to his office he thinks about Terri's breasts. They're splendid, of course. But he finds it curious that she will tell nearly anybody that they are, as we say, surgically enhanced. Last time he was in the dating pool back in the Pleistocene era, he never encountered anything but natural mammary glands. Then he got married and, ten years later, he's suddenly back in circulation and every woman he meets has gorgeous tits, but whenever he reaches for them he hears: 'Maybe I should mention that, they're, you know . . .' And inevitably, later: 'Listen, you're a doctor, do you think, I mean, there's been a lot of negative publicity and stuff . . .' It got so he avoided saying he was a doctor, not knowing whether they were genuinely interested or just hoping to get an opinion on this weird lump under the arm, *Right here, see?* Despite all the years of medical school and all the sleepless hours of his internship, he never really believed he was a doctor; he felt like a pretender, although he eventually discovered that he felt like less of a pretender on one hundred milligrams of Seconal.

The weather, according to the radio, is hot and hotting up. Kevin has the windows up and the climate control at sixty-eight. High between ninety-five and ninety-eight. Which is about as predictable as 'Stairway to Heaven' on Rock 101, the station that plays all 'Stairway,' only 'Stairway,' twenty-four hours a day – a song which one of the MD junkies in rehab insisted was about dope, but to a junkie everything is about dope. Now the song makes McClarty think of Terri marching righteously on her Stairmaster.

After a lifetime in Chicago he likes the hot summers and temperate winters, and he likes the ur-American suburban sprawl of franchises and housing developments with an affection all the greater for being self-conscious. As a bright, fatherless child he'd always felt alien and isolated; later as a doctor he felt even farther removed from the general populace – it's like being a cop – which alienation was only enhanced when he also became a drug addict and de facto criminal. He wanted to be part of the stream, an unconscious member of the larger community, but all the morphine in the pharmacy couldn't produce the desired result. When he first came out of rehab, after years of escalating numbness, the sight of a Burger King or a familiar television show could bring him to tears, could make him feel, for the first time, like a real *American*.

He turns into the drive marked MIDSTATE CORREC-TION FACILITY. It's no accident that you can't see the buildings from the road. With homes worth half a million within a quarter mile, construction was discreet. No hearings, since the land belonged to the state, which was happy to skip the expense of a new prison and instead board its high-security criminals with the corporation that employs Dr Kevin McClarty. He drives along the east flank of chain-link fence and triple-coiled concertina wire.

These guards, too, greet him by name and title when he signs in. Through the bulletproof Plexi he sees the enlarged photo of an Air Jordan sneaker a visitor just happened to be wearing when he hit the metal detector, its sole sliced open to show a .25-caliber Beretta nesting snug as a fetus in the exposed cavity. *Hey, it musta come from the factory that way, man, like those screws and syringes and shit that got inside the Pepsi cans, I ain't never seen that piece before. What is that shit, a twenty-five? I wouldn't be caught dead with no twenty-five, man, you can't stop a roach with that fucking popgun.*

Dr McClarty is buzzed through the first door and, once it closes behind him, through the second. Inside he can sense it, the malevolent funk of the prison air, the dread ambience of the dream. The varnished concrete floor of the long white hall is as shiny as ice.

Emma, the fat nurse, buzzes him into the medical ward.

'How many signed up today,' he asks.

'Twelve so far.'

McClarty retreats to his office, where Donnie, the head nurse, is talking on the phone. 'I surely do appreciate that . . . thank you kindly . . .' Donnie's perennially sunny manner stands out even in this region of pandemic cheerfulness. He says good morning with the accent on the first syllable, then runs down coming attractions. 'A kid beat up in D last night. He's waiting. And you know Peters from K block, the diabetic who's been bitching about the kitchen food? Saying the food's running his blood sugar up? Well, this morning they searched his cell and found three bags of cookies, a Goo Goo Cluster and two Moon Pies under the bed. I think maybe we should tell the commissary to stop selling him this junk. Yesterday his blood sugar was four hundred.'

Dr McClarty tells Donnie that they can't tell the commissary any such thing, that would be a restriction of Peters's liberty – cruel and unusual punishment. He'd fill out a complaint, and they'd spend four hours in court downtown, where the judge would eventually deliver a lecture, thirdhand Rousseau, on the natural Rights of Man.

Then there's Caruthers from G, who had a seizure and claims he needs to up his dose of Klonopin. Ah, yes, Mr Caruthers, we'd *all* like to up *that* and file the edges right off our day. In McClarty's case from zero milligrams a day to about twenty, with a little Demerol and maybe a Dilaudid thrown into the mix just to secure the perimeter. Or, fuck it, go straight for the fentanyl. No – he mustn't think this way. Like those 'impure thoughts' the priests used to warn us about, these pharmaceutical fantasies must be stamped out at all cost. He should call his sponsor, catch a meeting on the way home.

The first patient, Cribbs, a skinny little white kid, has a bloody black eye, which, on examination, proves to be an orbital fracture. That is, his eye socket has been smashed in. And while McClarty has never seen Cribbs before, the swollen face is familiar; he saw it last night in his sleep. 'Lock and sock?' he asks.

The kid nods and then winces at the pain.

'They just come in the middle of the night, maybe five of them, and started whaling on me. I was just lying there minding my own business.' Obviously new, he doesn't even know the code yet – not to tell nobody nothing. He is a sniveler, a skinny chicken, an obvious target. Now, away from his peers and tormentors, he seems ready to cry. But he suddenly wipes his nose and grins, shows McClarty the bloody teeth marks on his arm. 'One of the sonsofbitches bit me,' he says, looking incongruously pleased.

'You enjoyed that part, did you, Mr Cribbs?' Then, suddenly, McClarty guesses.

'That'll fix his fucking wagon,' says Cribbs, smiling hideously, pink gums showing above his twisted yellow teeth. 'I got something he don't want. I got the HIV.'

After McClarty cleans up the eye, he writes up a hospital transfer and orders a blood test.

'They won't be messing with me no more,' Cribbs says in parting. In fact, in McClarty's experience there are two approaches to AIDS cases among the inmate population. Many are indeed given a wide berth. Or else they are killed, quickly and efficiently and without malice, in their sleep.

Next is a surly, muscled black prisoner with a broken hand. Mr Brown claims to have smashed, accidentally, into the wall of the recreation yard. 'Yeah, playing handball, you know?' Amazing how many guys hurt themselves in the yard. Brown doesn't even try to make this story sound convincing; rather he turns up his lip and fixes McClarty with a look that dares him to doubt it.

So far, in the year he has worked here, McClarty has

been attacked only in his dreams. But he has been threatened several times, most recently by Lesko. A big pear-shaped redneck in for aggravated assault, he took a knife to a bartender who turned him away at closing time. The bartender was stabbed fifteen times before the bouncer hit Lesko with a bat. And while Lesko did threaten to kill McClarty, fortunately it wasn't in front of the other prisoners, in which case he would feel that his honor, as well as his buzz, was at stake. Still, McClarty makes a note to check up on Lesko; he'll ask Santiago, the guard over on D, to get a reading on his general mood and comportment.

Dr McClarty makes the first official phone call of the day, to a pompous ass of a psychopharmacologist to get an opinion on Caruthers's medication, not that McClarty doesn't have an opinion himself; he is required to consult a so-called expert. McClarty thinks Peganone would stave off the seizures just as effectively and more cheaply – which after all is his employer's chief concern – whereas Caruthers's chief concern, quite apart from his seizures, is catching that Klonopin buzz. Dr Withers, who has already talked to Caruthers's lawyer, keeps McClarty on hold for ten minutes, then condescendingly explains the purpose and methodology of double-blind studies, until McClarty is finally forced to remind the good doctor that he *did* attend medical school. In fact, he graduated second in his class at the University of Chicago. Inevitably they assume that a prison doctor is an idiot and a quack. In the old days McClarty would have reached through the phone and ripped this hick doctor's eyeballs out of his skull, asked him how he liked that for a double-blind study, but now he is content to hide out in his windowless office behind these three-foot-thick walls and let some other fucker find the cure for cancer. 'Thank you very much, *Doctor*,' McClarty finally says, cutting the old geek off midsentence.

Emma announces the next patient, Peters, the Moon Pie-loving diabetic, then slams the door in parting. A fat man with a jellylike consistency, Peters is practically bouncing on the examining table. Everything about him is soft and slovenly except his eyes, which are hard and sharp, the eyes of a scavenger ever alert to the scrap beneath the feet of the predators. The eyes of a snitch.

McClarty examines his folder. 'Well, Mr Peters.'

'Hey, Doc.'

'Any ideas why your blood sugar's up to four hundred?'

'It's the diabetes, Doc.'

'I guess it wouldn't have anything to do with that stash of candy found in your cell this morning?'

'I was holding that stuff for a friend. Honest.'

Another common refrain here in prison, this is a line McClarty remembers fondly from his drug days. It's what he told his mother the first time she found pot in the pocket of his jeans. The guys inside have employed it endlessly; the gun in the shoes or the knife or stolen television set always belongs to some other guy; they're just holding it for him. They never cease to profess amazement that the cops, the judge, the prosecutor, didn't believe them, that their own court-appointed lawyers somehow sold them out at the last minute. They are *shocked*. It's all a big mistake. *Honest. Would I lie to you, Doc?* They don't belong here in prison, and they are eager to tell you why. With McClarty it's just the opposite. He *knows* he belongs in here. He dreams about it. It is more real to him than his other life, than Terri's breasts, than the ailing lawn outside these walls. But somehow, inexplicably, every day they let him walk out the door at the end of his shift. And back at Live Oakes, the guards wave him through the gate inside the walls of that residential oasis as if he really were an upstanding citizen. Of course, technically he is not a criminal. The hospital did not bring charges, in return for his agreement to resign and go into treatment. On the other hand, neither the hospital administrators nor anybody else knew that it was he, McClarty, who had shot nurse Marcia DeVane full of the Demerol she craved so very dearly less than an hour before she drove her car into the abutment of the bridge.

Terri calls just before lunch to report that the caretaker thinks the brown spots on the lawn are caused by cat urine. 'I told him that's ridiculous, they're not suddenly peeing any more than they used to – oh, wait, gotta go. Kiss kiss. Don't forget about the Clausens, at seven. Don't worry, they're friends of Bill.' She hangs up before McClarty can tell her he might stop off at Unity Baptist on the way home.

Toward the end of the day McClarty goes over to Block D, to check the progress of several minor complaints. He is buzzed into the block by Santiago. 'Hey, Doc, what chew think about Aikman's straining his ankle? Your Cowboys, they gonna be hurtin' till he come back.' Santiago labors cheerfully under the impression that McClarty is a big

Dallas Cowboys fan, a notion that apparently developed after the doctor mumbled something to the effect that he really didn't pay much attention to the Oilers. McClarty has never followed sports, doesn't know Cowboys from Indians, but he is happy enough to play along, amused to find himself at this relatively late stage in life assigned to a team, especially after he heard the Cowboys referred to on television as 'America's team.' Like eating at McDonald's, it makes him feel as if he were a fully vested member of the Republic.

'Hey, Doc – that strain? That, like, a serious thing?'

'Could be,' McClarty says, able at last to offer a genuine opinion on his team. 'A sprain could put him out for weeks.'

Santiago is jovial and relaxed, though he is the only guard on duty in a cell block of twenty-four violent criminals, most of whom are on the block this moment, lounging around the television or conspiring in small knots. If they wanted to they could overpower him in a minute; it is only the crude knowledge of greater force outside the door of the block that keeps them from doing so. McClarty himself has almost learned to suppress the fear, to dial down the crackle of active malevolence which is the permanent atmosphere of the wards, as palpable as the falling pressure and static electricity before a storm. So he is not alarmed when a cluster of inmates moves toward him, Greco and Smithfield and two others whose names he forgets. They all have their ailments and their questions and they're trotting over to him like horses crossing the field to a swinging bucket of grain.

'Hey, Doc!' they call out from all sides. And once again,

he feels the rush that every doctor knows, the power of the healer, a taste of the old godlike sense of commanding the forces of life and death. This truly is the best buzz, but he could never quite believe it, or feel that he deserved it, and now he's too chastened to allow himself to really revel in the feeling. But he can still warm himself, if only briefly, in the glow of this tribal admiration, even in this harsh and straitened place. And for a moment he forgets what he has learned at such expense in so many airless smoky church basements – that he is actually powerless, that his healing skills, like his sobriety, are on loan from a higher power, just as he forgets the caution he has learned from the guards and from his own experience behind these walls, and he doesn't see Lesko until it is too late, fat Lesko who is feeling even nastier than usual without his Valium, his hand striking out from the knot of inmates like the head of a cobra, projecting a deadly thin silvery tongue. McClarty feels the thud against his chest, the blunt impact which he does not immediately identify as sharp-instrument trauma. And when he sees the knife he reflects that it's a damn good thing he is not Terri, or his left breast implant would be punctured. As he falls into Lesko's arms he realizes, with a sense of recognition bordering on relief, that he is back in the dream. They've come for him at last.

Looking up from the inmate roster, Santiago is puzzled by this strange embrace – and by the expression on McClarty's face as he turns toward the guard booth. 'He was smiling,' Santiago would say afterward, 'like he just heard a good one and wanted to tell it to you, you know, or like he was saying, *Hey, check out my bro Lesko here*.' Santiago told the same thing to his boss, to the board of inquiry, to the grand jury and to the prosecutor, and he would always tell the story to the new guards who trained under him. It never ceased to amaze him – that smile. And after a respectful pause and a thoughtful drag on his cigarette, Santiago would always mention that the doc was a big Cowboys fan.

SMOKE

THAT SUMMER IN NEW York everyone was wearing yellow ties. The stock market was coming into a long bull run; over plates of blackened redfish, artists and gourmet-shop proprietors exchanged prognostications on the Dow. And on the sidewalks noble dark men from Senegal were selling watches, jewelry and fake Gucci bags. No one seemed to know how or why these Africans had come to town – certainly not the police, who tried with little success to explain in English the regulations governing street vendors and finally sent out a special French-speaking squad, who received the same blank smiles. It was a mystery. Also that summer, Corrine and Russell Callahan quit smoking.

Russell Callahan was not one of those wearing a tie. He had worn a tie to work his first day at the publishing house and sensed suspicion among his colleagues, as if this had signaled aspirations to a higher position, or a lunch date with someone already elevated. The polite bohemian look of the junior staff suited him just fine, and abetted his belief that he was engaged in the enterprise of literature. On clear days he saw himself as an underpaid hack in a windowless annex of a third-rate institution. After two promotions he presided over a series of travel books composed of plagiarism and speculation in equal parts. The current title, *Grand Hotels of America*, was typical: he and his associates plundered the literature in print, sent letters requesting brochures and then wrote colorful and informative descriptions designed to convey the impression of eyewitness reporting. Certain adjectives became severely dog-eared in the process. The words *comfortable*, *elegant* and *spacious* encountered outside the office made Russell feel queasy and unclean. In May, a month after the current project had been launched, two years after he'd started work, he'd been assigned a college intern, an eager young woman named Tracey Wheeler. As a mentor, he found himself assuming the air of a grizzled veteran, and Tracey's enthusiasm helped to focus his cynicism about his job.

Corrine worked as an analyst in a brokerage house. If she had been a man, she would've had an easier time of it her first year. She nearly quit on several occasions. But once she became comfortable with the work, she found that the men around her were vaguely embarrassed by the old cigars-and-brandy etiquette, and vulnerable to the suspicion that she and her female colleagues possessed a new rule book. Gifted with mathematical genius and a wildly superstitious nature, she found herself precisely equipped to understand the stock market. She felt near the center of things. The sweat and blood of labor, the rise and fall of steel pistons, the test-tube match-making of chemicals and cells – all the productive energies of the world, coded in binary electronic impulses, coursed through the towers of downtown Manhattan, accessible to her at any moment on the screen of her terminal. Corrine came to appreciate aspects of a style that had at first intimidated her: she started playing squash again, and began to enjoy the leathery, wood-paneled, masculine atmosphere of the clubs where she sometimes lunched with her superiors, under the increasingly benign gaze of dead rich men in gilt frames.

Corrine and Russell had met in college. They were married the summer of graduation, and in New York their East Side apartment became a supper club for former classmates. As a married couple, the Callahans were pioneers of the state of adulthood, but they were also indulgent hosts. They put out crystal with dinner and weren't appalled if a piece of stemware got smashed toward morning. Men who had found Corrine daunting in college, when she was an erotic totem figure, could now flirt with her safely, while women often confided in Russell, drawing him into the bedroom for urgent conferences. He had been known as a poet in college, his verse tending toward the Byronic. Now people who'd hardly known him at school fished up from the yearbook file of their memories words like *sensitive* and *artistic* when his name was mentioned.

A Memorial Day party had reached the stage at which the empty glasses were becoming ashtrays when Nancy Tanner drew Russell into the bedroom. As she tugged him by his fingers, he watched the thick tongue of blond hair licking the back of her shoulders and the edge of her red dress, and remembered again something he'd thought of earlier – that he'd actually slept with her one night in college.

'I guess you've noticed I haven't exactly been myself tonight.'

She sat down on the bed and looked up at Russell, who thought that Nancy had been exactly herself, trolling her scooped neckline under the eyes of his friends, her laugh audible from any corner of the living room.

'My stepfather just went into the hospital with cancer. It's really got me down.'

'That's rough.' Russell didn't know what else to say, and Nancy seemed to be bearing up anyway.

'He used to take me to the Museum of Natural History. I always wanted to see the Eskimos, and I'd think how nice it would be to live in a little round igloo. I was a pretty ugly kid, but he'd call me his beauty queen.' Actual tears were welling in her eyes, and Russell began to believe that she was genuinely upset, and to feel guilty for doubting it.

'I haven't told anybody,' she said, reaching for his hand, which he surrendered. 'I just wanted you to know.'

'I find it hard to believe the part about your being an ugly kid,' Russell said, finally summoning some conviction. She wasn't nearly as good-looking as Corrine, he reminded himself, impressed with his own loyalty.

She stood up and dabbed at her eyes with her free hand. 'Thank you, Russell.' She leaned forward and kissed him. In temperature and duration it was a little beyond what the situation called for.

'Do you have a cigarette,' she asked when she drew away.

In the hallway Bruce Davidoff was pounding on the bathroom door. Seeing Russell, he said, 'Twenty minutes they've been in there.' Back in the living room Corrine was talking with Rick Cohen, cupping her hand in front of her to catch the ashes from her cigarette, nodding vigorously, her smoky exhalations dissipating like contrails of her rapid speech. He liked to watch her at parties, eavesdrop on her conversations with other men. At these times she seemed more like the woman he had proposed to than the one with whom he watched the eleven o'clock news.

'Symbols work in the market the same way they do in literature,' Corrine was saying.

Frowning earnestly, Rick Cohen said, 'I don't quite follow you there.'

Corrine considered, taking a thoughtful drag on her cigarette. 'There's, like, a symbolic order of things underneath the real economy. A kind of dream life of the economy that affects the market as much as the hard facts, the stats. The secret urges and desires of consumers and producers work up toward the surface. Market analysis is like dream interpretation. One thing stands for another thing – a new hairstyle means a rise in gold and a fall in bonds.'

Rick Cohen nodded to mask his incomprehension. Russell moved toward the kitchen to check out the wine situation. Except for Corrine, the perfect hostess, who was splitting the difference, it seemed to him that the publishing people were all talking about the stock market and the financial people were talking about books and movies. By the end of the night everyone would be talking about real estate – co-ops, condominiums, summer rentals in the Hamptons. Igloos on West Seventy-ninth Street. *Spacious, comfortable, elegant.*

After the last guest had been shoveled into the elevator, Corrine and Russell sat on the couch in the living room and had a cigarette before turning in. Russell put a side of Hank Williams on the stereo to wind them down. Corrine said, 'God, I'm tired. I don't think I can keep this up.'

'Keep what up?'

'Everything.' She stubbed out her butt and winced at the ashtray. 'We've got to quit smoking. I feel like I'm dying.'

Russell looked down at the cigarette between his fingers, as if it might suddenly show overt signs of hostility. He knew what she meant. It was a nasty habit. They had talked about quitting before, and Russell had always believed that someday they would.

'You're right,' he said. 'Let's quit.'

To mark the end of the smoking era, Corrine insisted, they should hunt up all the cigarettes in the apartment and break them into pieces. Russell would just as soon have waited till morning, but he got up and joined her in the ritual, leaving one pack in the pocket of a blazer in his closet for insurance.

As they were loading the dishwasher, she said, 'Phil Crane was hitting on me tonight.'

'What do you mean – "hitting on you"?'

'I mean he made it pretty clear that if I was interested, he was too.' She sounded sad, as if she'd lived in a world where until tonight infidelity hadn't existed.

'That son of a bitch. What did he say?'

'It doesn't matter.' She then added she was sorry she mentioned it, and made him promise he wouldn't say anything to Phil.

Later, in bed, she said, 'Have you ever been unfaithful?'

'Of course not,' he said, and then remembered Nancy Tanner in the bedroom.

Russell had first caught sight of Corrine at the top of a fraternity-house staircase, leaning forward over the banister with a cigarette in her fingers, looking down at a party that until that moment had seemed to Russell the climax of his recent escape from home and parents. He'd been drinking everything in sight, huddling with his new roommates, getting ridiculously witty at the expense of girls he was just working up the courage to talk to. Then he saw Corrine at the top of the stairs. He felt he knew her, everything essential in her character, though he'd never seen her before. He stifled his first impulse, to point her out to his roommates, not sure that they would see what he saw. Russell believed in his own secret aristocracy, a refinement of soul and taste which he had learned to keep to himself, and which much later he would almost cease to believe in. Later he would realize that most of us believe in our ability to read character from physiognomy. But now, while she ignored him from her aerie atop the staircase, he read intelligence into her eyes, breeding into her nose, sensuality into her lips, self-confidence into her languid pose. As he watched, a boy he recognized as a campus icon appeared on the landing behind her, along with another couple. She turned, and though he couldn't see her expression, though they didn't touch, the air of familiarity and possession between the two was unmistakable; and then both couples disappeared from view, retreating to the real party, the actual center of the world, an action that suddenly revealed the event on the lower floor to be a beer brawl, a congress of the second-rate.

The social and academic accomplishments of his first semester, unknown to Corrine, were committed in her name. He didn't have to sleuth hard for news of her, since she formed part of the group everyone talked about, which made her seem more desirable and less accessible, as did her liaison with Dino Signorelli. Signorelli was a basketball star and a druggie, a formidable combination. Tall, lanky and slightly bowlegged, he was alleged to be good-looking, although Russell disputed this judgment as he bided his time. He had four years.

Second semester Corrine was in his English class, and without ever actually meeting they became acquainted. At registration the next fall he ran into her coming out of the administration building and she greeted him as if they were friends. It was a hot September day. Russell admired the tan slopes of her legs, imagined that he could feel radiant heat from the waves of her long, dark hair. He kept waiting for her to say goodbye. She kept talking.

They talked through lunch at the Inn, filling the ashtray and emptying beer mugs. They talked about everything, but he couldn't stop thinking about her mouth, her lips on a cigarette, the clouds of smoke that she exhaled seeming to him the visible trace of inner fires. Still smoking and talking, they found themselves in Russell's dorm room, where they suddenly fell on each other – a crisis of lips and tongues and limbs which somehow stopped just short of the desired conclusion. She was still going with Dino, and he was involved with a girl named Maggie Sloan.

Their romance fell dormant for almost two years, till Corrine called up one night and asked if she could come over. She said she'd broken up with Dino, although she had failed to make this clear to Dino, who began calling up and then coming over to shout drunken threats across the quad soon after Corrine holed up in Russell's room. Although he was worried about Dino, Russell savored the atmosphere of siege, which lent an extra dimension of urgency, danger and illegitimacy to their union. He broke up with Maggie Sloan over the phone. Crying, Maggie appealed to the weight of tradition – the two years they'd been going out. Russell, with Corrine at his side, was sympathetic but firm.

Outside the dorm it was a prematurely cold New England fall; red and yellow leaves slipped from the trees and twisted in the wind. For three days they left the room only to get food, staying in bed most of the time, drinking St Pauli Girls, smoking Marlboros and talking. Russell had been a party smoker before, but Corrine smoked heavily, and Russell gradually caught up with her. They smoked before bed, after making love and then in the morning before they got out of bed, while Corrine told Russell her dreams in minute detail. Her imagination was curiously literal. She remembered everything – what people were wearing, inconsistencies and illogic that seemed to surprise and annoy her a little, as if she expected dreams not to be so dreamlike. Her view of the waking world, though, was somewhat fantastic. Certain dates and names were fraught with unlikely significance for her, and, much more than

Russell, the class poet, she believed in the power of words. When, after a week, Russell asked her to marry him, she made him solemnly promise never to use the word *divorce*, even in jest.

He might have taken her acceptance of his proposal to be impulsive, her renunciation of Dino to be precipitate, but he'd been in love with her for two and a half years.

The campus seemed to split down the middle over the issue. Some sided with the new couple, some with Maggie Sloan and Dino, whose senior basketball season was visibly affected. He became a loud and dangerous regular at the pub, and one night, while Corrine and Russell were at a movie, watching French people smoke cigarettes and cheat on each other, Dino trashed Russell's room. Corrine and Russell developed a repertoire of Dino jokes. The day of their wedding, in June, two weeks after graduation, Dino was in a car wreck that landed him in the hospital for three weeks. Two years after graduation they heard that he was working as a representative for a feed-and-grain distributor in South Dakota.

The morning after the Memorial Day party Corrine reminded Russell of their resolution, and for the first time since they'd known each other they had coffee without cigarettes. Russell left his first cup unfinished.

Corrine was staring wistfully at her blue Trivial Pursuit coffee mug. Somebody had given them a set of four for a wedding present – Russell tried to recall who it was. 'Remember that Campbell's soup commercial?' she said. 'Soup and sandwich, love and marriage, horse and carriage?'

Russell nodded. 'They forgot caffeine and nicotine.'

'I've heard it helps to drink a lot of water the first few days,' Corrine said. 'Cleans out the system.'

Russell got half a glass of water down before he had to leave for work. 'We've got to buy you some new shirts,' Corrine said, fingering Russell's frayed collar when they were in the elevator.

'I've got plenty of shirts,' Russell said.

'We can certainly afford a few more,' Corrine said.

One of us can, Russell thought.

At a little after eleven Corrine called him at the office.

'How are you holding up?'

'All I can think about is cigarettes.'

'Me too.'

Talking about it made it easier. Or else it made it harder. They weren't sure, but agreed to call each other whenever they were feeling weak. Tracey Wheeler, Russell's intern, came over with a set of galleys she had proofread, smoking a cigarette; she must have seen him looking at it longingly.

'Do you want one?'

'No,' he said. 'I've quit. At least I'm trying.' He felt sad hearing himself. The words seemed to mark the end of a chapter in his life, and made him feel older, relative to Tracey, in a way he didn't like. It sounded fussy, not at all in keeping with the swashbuckling air he assumed whenever she was around.

After Corrine hung up the phone, Duane Jones, an analyst, who'd gone through training with her, came into the office and sat down. Corrine and Duane had made a habit of stealing a midmorning break together. This ritual had developed in part because they had been the only smokers in the training program. The first day of orientation she had done mental caricatures of the faces around the seminar table. Duane was GQ subscriber, Dartmouth class officer, boxer shorts and jockstraps, lacrosse and skiing. The fact that he smoked made him seem less buttoned-down. Now they often had lunch together, to the point that Russell was a little jealous. Russell always referred to Duane as 'Dow Jones, Industrious Average.' Duane called him 'the Poet.' This morning Duane sat down on the edge of the armchair across from the desk and adjusted one of his socks.

'Got any brilliant hunches this morning? Any dreams that might have a bearing on the Exchange?' He took out a new pack of Merits and slapped it against his wrist.

'Put out a heavy sell call on tobacco issues. We quit smoking.'

'Say it ain't so. *You?*'

'Me and Russell both,' she said, not certain whether she was being loyal or laying off part of the blame on her husband.

Duane stood up and straightened his yellow tie. 'I won't tempt you,' he said. At the door he turned and winked. 'But if you change your mind . . .'

That night Corrine cooked a deliberately bland meal of chicken, peas and rice. It was the first time they'd eaten at home in weeks. Corrine had read somewhere that red meat and spicy food aggravated the craving to smoke.

'I think we should try not to go out so much for a while,' Corrine said, as they ate in front of the television. They were watching a rerun of *M*A*S*H*; Hawkeye was wooing a recalcitrant nurse.

'Have you noticed that on television hardly anyone smokes?' Russell asked.

Corrine nodded. 'Moratorium on French movies.'

'Absolutely.'

'And it wouldn't hurt us to cut down on our drinking.'

Russell agreed in principle, even as the ice shrank in his third drink of the evening. After ten hours of not smoking he had arrived home feeling like he'd been beaten up, and had reached immediately for the vodka.

Russell said, 'The old soup-and-sandwich theorem.'

'The thing we've got to realize,' Corrine said, 'is that you can't have "just one cigarette." If you break down once, you'll do it more easily the next time.'

'Right.' Russell was trying to watch *M*A*S*H*. Corrine had absolutely no television etiquette. She would talk through the first twenty-five minutes of a show and then ask Russell to explain what was going on. Her questions were a little maddening at the best of times. Tonight he was ready to hurl her out the window. Either that or grab the pack of smokes he'd left in his blazer in the closet.

'Russell?'

'Yeah?'

'Please listen just for one minute. This is important.'

He looked at her. She was wearing her earnest, small-girl-wanting-to-know-why-the-sky-is-blue expression. He normally found this look devastating.

'Did you ever,' she said, 'when you were a kid, pretend that something really bad would happen to you if you did or didn't do something? You know, like if you didn't stay

113

underwater till the far end of the pool, then somebody would die?'

'All the time,' Russell said. 'Thousands died.'

'I'm serious. Let's pretend, like that, that something really bad will happen to us if we start smoking again.'

'Okay,' Russell said, turning back to the TV.

The next day Corrine screamed at Russell for leaving his dirty socks in the bathroom sink. He got mad at her when he went to the kitchen and found the cupboards bare: How was he supposed to quit smoking if he couldn't have some toast or cereal to keep his mouth busy? She said the shopping wasn't her responsibility – she certainly brought home her share of the grocery money. Corrine stormed out of the house without saying goodbye, forgetting her briefcase. At the office Russell bummed a cigarette from Tracey and almost smoked it out of spite, as a way of getting back at Corrine. He finally broke it in half and threw it in the wastebasket.

That night, when Corrine got home, their fight was not mentioned; they were both shy and solicitous, as if helping each other through a tropical illness. They cranked up the air-conditioning and collapsed into bed at ten. Russell woke up at seven with a keen sensation of guilt. Corrine was not in bed; he heard the shower running in the bathroom. Gradually he began to recall a dream: He'd been at a party, and Nancy Tanner was beckoning to him from the door of an igloo. The purpose of the invitation was unclear. Russell walked toward the open door. It was surprisingly distant, and with each step he told himself he should turn around and run. When he finally reached her, she held out a cigarette and smiled lewdly.

Corrine came into the bedroom wearing a towel twisted around her head and another secured beneath her arms.

'We've got to do something about this water pressure,' she said, sitting down at the vanity. Lying in bed, Russell could see her face in the mirror as she began to apply her makeup. She caught his eye and smiled. 'What are you so serious about?'

'Nothing.'

'I had the weirdest dream last night,' she said.

'What else is new,' he said, glad that she was accustomed to his not remembering his own dreams.

'I dreamed about cigarettes. Sneaking a smoke, like when I was a kid.'

Applying a tool shaped like a miniature toothbrush to her eyebrow, she said, 'Have you dreamed about it?' Her eyes zoomed in on his for just a moment, and reflexively he answered. 'No.'

'I guess I'm just perverse.'

The next night Corrine dreamed that she was standing on the sidewalk, waiting for someone. The street was entirely deserted, though it was Park Avenue. Not another soul on the sidewalk, not a car on the street. A black limousine appeared several blocks down, cruising toward her slowly, finally pulling up and stopping by the curb in front of her. The glass was smoked; she couldn't see inside the car. The back window slipped down; a man's hand emerged from the open window, holding out a pack of cigarettes. She looked up and down the street, and then climbed into the limo. She couldn't make out the figure beside her in the backseat, but as the car pulled away from the curb, she saw Russell looking down from a window in an apartment building high above the street.

In the morning she didn't mention the dream. Getting Russell's attention had been difficult lately anyway.

That week was the first real scorcher of the summer; the humidity brimmed to the verge of rain, without breaking. Walking to the subway the next morning, Corrine could feel her damp blouse sticking to her shoulderblades. In the station the men in yellow ties looked wilted, the women in their tailored suits defensive, as if they sensed that on days like this the subterranean violence of the city was likely to boil to the surface. She had forgotten to buy a paper, and as her gaze wandered idly around the platform, she suddenly met the eyes of a ragged man staring back at her with malevolent intensity. She turned away, staggered by that look, her mind unreeling images of carnage: muzzle flash, neon blood, filthy hands at her throat, boldface headlines. As the train rattled in, she couldn't help looking again; this time she saw a blank face and lusterless, unfocused eyes behind a tangle of matted hair.

A little after ten Duane Jones stuck his head into her office. 'Still being virtuous?'

She motioned him in and whispered, 'Close the door.'

He raised his eyebrows and pulled the door closed.

'Let me have a couple of drags.'

'All this secrecy for a couple of drags?'

'Just light it, will you?'

He shook a Merit out of his pack and held it out to her.

116

'No, you light it.'

Duane was enjoying this. He lit the cigarette with his lighter and held it out to her. 'The idea being that if I light it, you won't have actually smoked a cigarette?'

'Humor me.' She took the cigarette and inhaled deeply, held the smoke in her lungs. 'Funny, it doesn't taste like I thought it would.'

'You look great with a cigarette.'

She took another, strictly experimental drag. This was more like what she had anticipated, a reunion clinch with a former lover. But she wasn't going to hop into bed. She just wanted to remind herself that she could live without this one passion. Corrine held the cigarette out to him, fortified with a new resolve. 'Take it.'

'I've got more.'

'Take it.'

'Okay.' Duane noted the faint peach impression of Corrine's lips on the filter. He took a drag.

Corrine was sorting papers on her desk, suddenly all business. 'I'm going to be here till midnight if I don't get moving,' she said.

'You know where to find me,' Duane said as he left.

The stock market was getting hot; Corrine was working twelve- and fourteen-hour days. With the advent of Tracey, Russell's workload was considerably lighter, but because of Corrine's job they couldn't get out of the city much. At first he enjoyed being able to meet friends for drinks, watch TV or read at home without interruption, though as the summer wore on, he began to resent her scrupulous fidelity to her job. One hot night when she arrived home after midnight, he made insinuations, mentioning Duane Jones.

At the office he read the *Times* front to back before settling into his official chores, and sometimes composed fake guide entries for his own amusement. One morning, as the temperature climbed toward ninety and the air-conditioning became less and less a source of relief, he was writing one of these when Tracey came in with a new batch of her own vivid compositions.

'I think I've finished Michigan,' she said. 'What state are you working on?'

He read: '"The Yukon Sheraton: charming, individual guest cottages constructed by native craftsmen of local materials; cozy interiors, domed ceilings, blubber heat. Year-round winter sports."'

She forced a faint, nervous chuckle, and then became pensive. 'Do you mind if I ask you something? Don't you think what we're doing is kind of, uh, unethical?'

'Think of yourself as a fiction writer.'

'I just feel funny about it.'

'Why do you think most of the senior staff is alcoholic?' This hard-boiled manner had become reflexive when he was talking with Tracey. He couldn't seem to be straightforward.

An inner struggle was working havoc on Tracey's normally cheerful demeanor. Russell couldn't help admiring the contours of her sleeveless top. 'It's just, you're so talented,' she gasped, as if delivering a horrible confession. She looked down at the floor. 'I'm being a baby.' She turned and walked out of the office. Russell stared at the door long after she had gone, then left early for lunch.

Lately Russell had felt a great shroud of gauze enveloping him, preventing him from touching life and getting hold of it. He felt torpid and cloudy, but didn't know whether this was a function of the oppressive weather, his decision to quit cigarettes or some subheading under Changes of Life.

Nicotine withdrawal seemed to dull his mind and sharpen all his senses. The rancid smells of the summer streets had never seemed so acute. The vapors curling from mysterious apertures in the city streets were cruel reminders. Where there's smoke, he thought. He ate four or five times a day. Even his hearing seemed sharper: noise bothered him, as if he were suffering from an extended hangover. And the women in their summer dresses on the sidewalks excited fantasies more detailed than any he'd experienced since adolescence.

On the way back from the coffee shop he walked two blocks out of his way to follow a redhead in a yellow halter top. He entertained the notion of striking up a conversation, but then she walked out of his life, slipping smartly into the revolving door of an office building.

'What the hell is wrong with you?' he said aloud, standing in the middle of the sidewalk, drawing scrutiny from several pedestrians who seemed ready to offer opinions.

He absolutely had to have a cigarette.

Outside the newsstand he stopped and reminded himself that he had already betrayed Corrine once today, if only in his imagination. He walked on, smokeless and repentant.

Waiting for a traffic light on the way back to the office, he looked over the display of a sidewalk vendor, one of those West Africans he'd read about in the *Times*, and spotted among the wares a cigarette case made out of python skin. Tracey would be leaving soon to go back to school. He bought the case for ten bucks and took it back to work. Tracey was at her desk, eating a bowl of cottage cheese.

'It's beautiful,' she said. 'You're so thoughtful.'

'It comes with strings attached,' Russell said.

She looked up warily.

'Give me a cigarette, for Christ's sake, before I die.' He smoked it in her cubicle. They talked about her courses for the fall. Russell wished he were going back to college, wished that he were embarking on some open-ended adventure, as he savored what he told himself would be his last cigarette.

One morning toward the end of August, Corrine woke up at 5 a.m. in a terrible state. She'd had a dream – the apartment had gone up in flames. Her breath was short, and she was trembling. At first she wanted to stay home from work, and wanted Russell to stay with her, but Russell pointed out that if the fire were in the apartment building, they were both better off in their offices.

She called after lunch to see if he was okay. As he was leaving the office, he called to remind her about a cocktail party that night. The theme was *La Mort d'Été*; for some reason all the parties had themes that year, as if conviviality were no longer its own reward.

'I won't be able to make it,' she said. 'You should go.'

'Got a previous engagement?' Russell suggested.

'Don't be an idiot, okay? It's been a bitch of a day already.'

'What should I wear?' Russell said.

'Wear a tie. They won't recognize you.'

'Remind me what you look like, so I'll recognize you when you get home tonight.'

'I'll be the girl with dark circles under her eyes.'

After a moment Russell said. 'How's old Dow Jones?'

'The market's up four points.'

'I mean the stiff with the starched boxer shorts.'

'Duane is very busy, like the rest of us.'

'I don't hear you denying my surmise about his under-shorts.'

'Would you like me to check?'

'No, that's okay.'

'I'll see you when I get home. And no smoking.'

Russell planned to make a quick appearance, but after two hours the party was just hitting optimal cruise altitude. The invitation said *Cocktails six to eight*, but food and booze were plentiful and everyone was canceling dinner reservations. Rick Cohen had some blow that he let Russell in on. By ten Russell had bummed three cigarettes. He felt guilty about the first. The second came after he visited the bathroom with Rick, and obviously that didn't count. Smoking the third, he decided that he was glad Corrine wasn't with him: he could be weak without spoiling her resolution.

Nancy Tanner arrived wearing one of her strapless dresses. She was flashy in a way that reminded him of stewardesses – a stylized, overly wrought femininity that he associated with the service sector. Her obviousness made him feel virtuous. If Nancy were a film, she'd be *Superman II*. Corrine was, say, *Hiroshima, Mon Amour*.

Nancy spotted Russell and winked, then caught up with him at the bar. 'Behaving yourself?' she asked.

'Trying.'

'Haven't seen you since . . . you remember.'

For a moment he thought she meant the dream. 'How's your stepfather?' he said.

'My stepfather?' She looked baffled for a moment. 'Oh, he's fine. He's better. Where's Corrine?' she asked, the way one asks after a tagalong sibling who has finally been given the slip. He felt that if he didn't challenge her tone in some way, he would be implicated in a developing conspiracy.

'Working,' he said.

'All work and no play . . .' She arched her eyebrows and then escaped before he could register his indignation. That was going a little too far. He got a drink and plunged back into the crowd.

'We were just wondering what happened to Dino Signorelli,' Rick said when Russell joined his circle.

'Last I heard, he was selling seeds in South Dakota.'

'Spilling seed, you mean,' Tom Dalton said.

'That guy could fake a guard like nobody's business.'

'He could bend an elbow, too,' Russell observed.

Russell was listening to Skip Blackman's girlfriend – who had never looked so good – talk about her incredibly boring job when Nancy touched his shoulder.

'Got a cigarette?'

Russell was about to say he'd quit, but deftly turned the reflex into a negative monosyllable.

'Let's find some,' she said, her eyes sparkling in a way that seemed to make this simple notion witty and daring.

She took his hand and he followed her, feeling crisp and purposeful in his movements, negotiating the tight throng of bodies and the carpeted floor like an expert skier rounding the poles of a hazardous slalom course.

'I think I've got some in my coat,' she said, leading him into one of the bedrooms. She closed the door behind them. He reached for her and drew her face to his, his feeling of precision and control dissolving, the ski slope giving way to a free fall through the clouds.

Shortly before midnight Russell reeled toward home. His legs were wobbly, but this was a transparent defensive strategy, a white lie on the part of the body on behalf of the guilty mind. It didn't work. His head was utterly clear, an acoustically perfect amphitheater for the voices of accusation. He told himself that it could have been worse; they hadn't closed the deal, those few minutes in the bedroom. But they might have. They were well on their way when somebody came in looking for a coat.

He took off his shoes in the hallway, eased the keys into the locks. The apartment was dark. He crept to the bedroom, which was empty. He tried to feel relief, told himself he had a second chance. He couldn't have faced Corrine tonight. She would have seen right through him.

Russell was in bed when he heard the stealthy ticking of keys and tumblers. With one eye half open he watched the door of the bedroom. The hallway remained dark. Eventually he heard her tiptoe into the bedroom; accustomed to the dark, he could see that she was carrying her shoes.

He pretended to be asleep as she undressed and slipped into bed beside him. He wanted to take her in his arms.

Corrine lay very still beside him. He waited for her rapid breathing to resolve itself into the rhythm of sleep; she could fall asleep on a dime. Instead her breath became shorter, more irregular, until he realized that she was crying. Somehow she knew. Russell cursed himself for violating this intimacy, which over the years had become so finely tuned that she was able, even in the silent dark, to sense a change in pitch. Then he decided that was absurd. He began to wonder where she'd been all night.

'Oh, Russell,' she said. 'I'm sorry.'

He lifted himself on an elbow and tried to see her face in the dark.

'What do you mean, you're sorry?'

She began to sob. Her back was heaving. She was trying to say something, but her words were muffled by the pillow.

'What?' he said.

When she finally spoke, it was in a dull, featureless voice that he had never heard before. 'Tonight,' she said, 'tonight I had a couple of cigarettes . . .'

She said more, but the sound of her voice was already fading away as Russell lay back on his own pillow, feeling the chill blast of the air conditioner on his face, imagining himself henceforth as a wanderer of frozen landscapes, and in searching for a suitably tragic picture of himself he came at length, unexpectedly, upon the image of Dino Signorelli, standing alone on a treeless prairie, hatless, leaning into the cold wind.

GETTING IN TOUCH WITH LONNIE

JARED LET HIS PARCHED eyes slide across the soothing green lawns, watched the impeccable houses sail past the cab window. Colonials, mostly – the indigenous style here in Protestant-refugee country – some dating all the way back to the exodus from the Old World. The twisty roads, paved and widened deer paths, the old stone walls, the deep green shade of oak and maple – all this was second nature to him. After two years, he wondered if he would ever become comfortable with palm trees and the architectural miscegenation of Los Angeles. In fact, he was thinking of moving back East. A town like this, maybe. He didn't have to live in Manhattan any more than he had to live in LA. They would come to him now. Send a car (with a bar and a phone, please). He regretted not hiring a car and driver in Manhattan for the round-trip, but had thought Laura would consider it ostentatious. He could've made some calls on the way up. One thing he had to do was call Lonnie. That was one thing you got used to in LA, car phones. The phone he could live without, but this cab he'd picked up at the train station seemed to date back to the Frank Capra era. Jared felt he was suffering some kind of serious chiropractic malpractice, between the springs sticking through the back seat and the potholes whose regular shocks seemed to travel directly up his spinal column without being even faintly absorbed.

Laura had tried to persuade him to move out to Connecticut a few years back, to the kind of place they'd both grown up in. And now she's finally made it back to the suburbs, he thought, feeling clever for just a moment, then guilty.

The cabdriver kept looking up into the rearview mirror. Jared was becoming familiar with, but by no means tired of, that particular look.

'Hey, excuse me – but aren't you that actor?'

Jared nodded, his manner at once shy and weary.

'Yeah, I thought you were. Don't tell me. What's your name?'

Jared told him.

'Right, that's it. All *right*. You were in that movie.'

'Been in a few,' Jared noted.

'How about that? This is great. I woke up this morning, I had a feeling something was gonna happen today. You know what I mean?'

'I had the same feeling,' Jared said.

'So, you checking into the Valley,' the driver asked.

It took Jared a minute to understand the question. Then he said, 'Me? No, I'm not checking in. I'm just visiting my . . . I'm visiting someone.'

'Hey, no offense. Lots of famous people come through here. In fact, this place is kind of famous for that. Of course, they come here so they can, you know, have their privacy. No publicity. I could tell you some names, man.'

'Well, I'm afraid I'm just visiting,' Jared said.

'Okay, sure. Listen, do you think you could sign your autograph for my kid?'

They pulled up a long, tree-lined driveway to a cluster of buildings which once might have composed the estate of a prosperous gentleman farmer, or a small New England prep school – a Georgian mansion surrounded by white clapboard satellites on several acres of blue-green lawn. Hard to believe this haven was just over an hour from the city. After only a day and a half back in Manhattan he remembered how compressed and accelerated life could be. Exhausting. Living in New York was like being on location for a movie that never wrapped.

God, I'm wiped, he thought, which reminded him that he needed to call Lonnie. Of course he wasn't sure if Lonnie was even in town.

Signing his autograph on the back of a taxi receipt, he heard his name called out. Laura was waving from the door of one of the houses, a large black woman beside her. Jared strode across the striped lawn, the two women coming out to meet him. Thinner than ever, Laura threw her arms around him and squeezed as hard as she was able. When she finally came up for air, he saw that the worry creases across her forehead had deepened. It had been four months since he'd seen her. She was still beautiful in her distress, a tall and elegant if rather too angular brunette. Her eyes fastened onto his, tugging at him, asking for answers to all of her questions. As a kid

Jared had been terrified by an old, supposedly bottomless quarry near his house, and that image often came to mind when he thought about the depth and vastness of Laura's need. She required so much love, her childhood stunted by some sort of emotional malnutrition, and he'd grown more and more unhappy and, finally, angry as he discovered his inability to deliver enough of it. Somehow, the worse he felt, the worse he behaved.

'This is Dorene,' Laura said, drawing back to indicate the companion at her elbow. 'Dorene's my special.'

'Your what?'

'She's like my nurse. She stays with me.'

Jared shook Dorene's hand, then glanced back at Laura. 'All the time?'

'No, of course not. She's with me from seven to three, and from three to eleven another nurse comes on. Then there's the night shift.'

'You have somebody sleep with you?'

'She sits in the chair beside the bed.'

'This is all so . . .' Jared halted, then nodded and tried to smile.

Laura nodded and shrugged. 'They think I'm still suicidal. I don't know. Some days I am.' She looked down at the ground. 'Sorry,' she said. 'I know it's tremendously expensive.' Though her face and her voice had been animated for a moment with the excitement of seeing him, she spoke now in the barely audible monotone he had come to know over the phone this past month.

'Forget it,' Jared said, happy that there was something he could feel noble about. The fact he was paying for this made him feel a little less guilty about everything that had happened. She had said it wasn't his fault, really, that all of the demons of her childhood had broken out of their cages at once, that it went back way before him. Her sadness over the dissolution of their marriage was just one more thing – not the sole cause of this acute depression which had finally required hospitalization. Meanwhile, his friends told him that no one can be entirely responsible for the happiness of another human being. Still . . .

Jared felt he should lighten the mood, particularly with a stranger hovering a few feet away. 'You know, Dorene,' he said in a phony-sounding drawl, 'ever since I was a kid I always thought I was kind of special. But it must be nice to *know* you're a special.'

It was weak, he knew, but she rewarded him with a smile anyway.

'You want to see my room,' Laura asked.

'Great,' he said, and together the three of them started across the grass back to the house. Suddenly remembering, Jared reached into the pocket of his jacket and handed Laura a small, gift-wrapped package.

'I'm afraid I'll have to open that,' Dorene said, reaching for it quickly. Suddenly she smiled a little sheepishly and returned the box to Laura. 'Sorry, it's just rules. But I don't suppose just this once . . .'

'Thanks,' Jared said, looking her in the eyes.

'I sure liked that movie of yours.'

Laura stopped walking, bringing them all to an abrupt and awkward halt. 'Take it,' she said, holding out the box to Dorene. 'Go ahead, take it. Rules are rules.' Reluctantly Dorene reclaimed it.

'This is my tiny little part of the world,' Laura said to

him. 'It's not much. But the funny farm's all I've got right now. You have the rest of America. So please don't try to charm everyone right off the goddamn bat, okay?'

Laura had decorated the room with her old stuffed animals, a number of framed photographs, including two of Jared, and several painted baskets he'd never seen. Two windows overlooked the woods and a stream. A hospital bed with metal railings provided the institutional note.

Sitting on the bed beside Jared, Laura opened her gift, a bottle of Chanel perfume. 'It's Number Nineteen,' she said.

'Your fave,' he said.

'I can't stand Nineteen. It's Number Five I like.'

'Are you sure?'

'Of course I'm sure. I hate Number Nineteen.' She threw the bottle down, and Dorene quietly retrieved it from the carpet.

'I'd swear it was Nineteen you liked,' he said.

'One of your other girls,' Laura said.

Jared had bought her the stuff for years, and couldn't believe he would forget. But there had been several Chanel purchases since he and Laura were together.

'Wait a minute, for Christ's sake. Remember a week ago, when I told you I was flying to London for that awards thing and we discussed how I should call Tony and Brenda and Ian and Carol and on and on, and when I called a couple nights later you said, "What are you doing in London?" After we'd talked about it for half an hour?'

'So? I'm sorry, my short-term memory's not so hot. The doctors said it was a symptom of the depression.'

'So maybe you forgot what number perfume you like.'

'Jared, you're unbelievable. You could talk yourself off death row and steal the warden's wife on your way out.'

'Never worked on you,' Jared said, wondering if the nurse was used to witnessing these sorts of scenes.

'Unfortunately it still does,' Laura said. 'I want you back.'

'What are you, crazy?' he said, unsure if he were trying to deflect the sudden seriousness of this meeting by hamming it up.

She held out her palms, indicating the room. 'It would appear so.'

'This is Wharton House,' Laura said, stopping in front of one of the largest houses in the complex. 'The substance-abuse facility.'

Jared nodded.

'I wanted you to see it. It's modeled on Hazelden, and supposedly it's a really successful program. You'd like a lot of the people in there. Writers, actors, professors. There's this one guy I really want you to meet. Rob – amazing guy. He's made a fortune on Wall Street – '

'Why in the world would I want to meet a *stock*broker?' Jared said, gently tugging at Laura's elbow in hopes of accelerating their tour of the grounds.

'I don't know, I just thought of you the minute I met him. He's got these eyes like yours. Anyway, he's in for cocaine. Used to deal to all these stars besides running his own investment firm. He's had an incredible life, lived with that model who's on the cover of *Cosmo* all the time and then – '

'You hate people like that, Laura.'

'Eventually he started going to Colombia to buy quantity himself, so he gets busted and put in jail in Cartagena. But within two weeks he has these mercenaries blow up the jail and smuggle him out of the country. Anyway, I think you'd like him. He's really smart.'

'If I told you about this guy, you'd say he sounds like an asshole.'

'He's charming. And besides, I admire his courage in coming here. That takes even more guts than breaking out of jail.'

'Sounds like love.'

'No,' she said. 'Except insofar as he reminds me of you.'

'That's one of the things I've missed about you,' Jared said. 'The way you use *insofar as* in conversation. Or *ergo*. We don't get that out in LA much. Anyway, I've never been to jail or Cartagena, either one.'

''Bout time we headed up for lunch,' said Dorene.

On the walk up the drive to the main house, they were joined by some of Laura's housemates. Eric, whom Laura had mentioned several times on the phone, was a gentleman of sixty and a professor of religion at Yale. He was not visibly depressed or sedated.

'Has Laura told you she's our best basket maker,' Eric asked.

'I'm an arts-and-crafts hero,' Laura said. 'I'm thinking of opening up a crafts boutique after I get out of here. Call it the Basket Case.'

After they moved through the cafeteria line, Laura introduced Jared around the table.

'Just arrive today?' said Tony, a young man with a scimitar-shaped scar across his throat.

Jared nodded, his mouth full of cold, tough veal.

'Where are you, Wharton House?'

'I'm just visiting,' Jared said.

'He's my husband,' Laura explained.

'Oh, I see.'

Jared wondered if the man was perhaps making a point by pretending not to know who he was.

The talk around the table was of the food and pharmacopoeia – prescribed dosages of antidepressants and lethal dosages of self-administered medication. Connie, a recently admitted middle-aged housewife – blonde and seemingly cheerful – had tried to kill herself with Valium, thirty of the five-milligram yellows. But she threw up, and everyone told her it wouldn't have done the trick anyway.

'Thirty of the blues might possibly have done it,' Jared added, eliciting a fairly general agreement around the table. 'Thirty Seconals would do the trick. But for real sledgehammer results, Dilaudids are your best bet. Thirty of those would kill you and your two best friends plus their household pets.' That got a laugh. 'Three thousand in the water supply would take out a medium-sized city.' Then in Ronald Reagan's voice, he said, 'The hell with nuclear weapons, you damn Commies, we got the neuron bomb.'

Everyone laughed except Laura, whose eyes he avoided.

Jackson, a Unitarian minister, told how he had closed his garage door, climbed into the Oldsmobile, inserted a tape in the cassette player and hit the ignition. When the tape turned over for the second play and he found himself still conscious, if nauseous, he gave up and went back into the house.

'It was a new car, a 1988,' he said. 'The new emissions-control systems are so good you can't even kill yourself.'

'What was the tape?' Laura said.

'Pachelbel.'

'Good choice. I love the Chaconne.'

'Thank you, Laura.'

Laura's approach to the world had always been slightly skewed. Was that a function of the imbalances that had landed her here, or just her charming eccentricity? Jared loved her, was still unable to divorce her after almost two years of separation. Sometimes he suspected he was afraid to let go because she was the only person who wouldn't allow him to reinvent himself completely, into something bright and shiny and superficial. So many old friends had been replaced by new ones. Laura was perhaps his last chance to remember and preserve the best of what he had been. On the other hand, was success such a crime? Everybody changes, so why did she insist that he was both selling and destroying his soul? At worst he was just visiting Babylon on a round-trip ticket. Which reminded him.

'Gotta make a quick call,' he told the company. 'Keep the veal patties cold for me, guys. I'll be right back.'

Jared was directed to a phone booth, where he used his credit card to call Lonnie's New York number. He listened through ten rings, then another ten. Strange, he thought, that Lonnie didn't have his machine turned on, but he probably was still asleep and had the phone unplugged.

'What was the phone call,' Laura asked as they were walking back to her house, Dorene trailing behind.

This, he remembered, was one of the things he hated – the suspicion.

'My agent,' he said. 'I can never get right through to him.'

'Just try and give me these few hours, Jared, will you? You'll be back in the world soon enough.'

'You're right. Okay, I'm sorry.'

She took his hand and squeezed it. 'I'm sorry Rob wasn't at lunch,' she said. 'I really wanted you guys to meet.'

'Who?'

'Rob. The ex-drug dealer.'

'Next time, then.'

'Can you come back soon?'

'Real soon. I gotta be in LA for a week or so, but I can get back right after that. It's for a part,' he added, seeing her disappointment.

They sat on lawn chairs in front of the house, and Jared feared a Serious Talk was coming on. But Dorene's presence made that unlikely. Laura reached out to take his hand again, and looked into his eyes as tears welled up in her own.

'Oh, Jared, I feel like I'm just this insignificant speck on this rock that's spinning through cold space. If nobody cares about any of us, why should I keep on living?'

'I care.'

'Not enough. Not more than anything. Not enough to come back.'

'Your hand's trembling,' Jared said.

'It's the lithium.' She withdrew her hand and looked

at his arm dangling over the arm of the lawn chair. 'So's yours,' she said. 'I noticed earlier.'

He looked at it skeptically. 'Jet lag.'

'Oh, come on, Jared.'

'I'm working too hard to be abusing myself,' he said.

'You always tap your foot when you tell a lie.'

'I'm trying to help with *your* problems,' he said. 'I'm functioning quite well out there, thanks.'

After a sullen silence they began to talk again, about her doctors and her therapy and eventually, as the sun dropped in the sky and Jared became used to Dorene's presence and the suburban lawn came to resemble other suburban lawns, they talked about their families and the old friends, the people who'd been at the wedding five years before in her parents' backyard.

For a moment Jared imagines that he and Laura might make a nice life of it, buying one of these big old white houses with fireplaces everywhere, starting a garden, cruising into the city for the theater and dinner. In a way, to surrender to the gentle yoke of domestic life would be such a relief. He knows Laura wanted children – and he does too, before very long. And she'd told him about some decent fly-fishing water somewhere in the vicinity. But even now another world is calling out to Jared, from beyond the stone walls and shaded lanes. Down the railroad tracks, south across a river, he can almost hear the buzz that begins anew every night – the clatter of silver and glassware and female voices busy with his praise . . .

Laura's asking him a question – repeating a question, in fact – about when he will be back. But just then he sees a man coming across the lawn. And when Laura turns to look at the man, her face lights up. He is tall, a younger man, although his posture seems weary, his gait heavy. The face is familiar, yet in this unfamiliar context it takes Jared a moment to identify it.

He stands up. 'Lonnie?'

'Hello, Jared,' the man answers.

'Lonnie? No, this is Rob,' Laura says. 'The guy I wanted you to meet.'

'We've met,' Rob says. And it's true. Jared's impulse is to flee across the lawn, but he doesn't feel he can move.

And the man he knows as Lonnie and has met many times, this man says, 'Welcome.'

HOW IT ENDED

I LIKE TO ASK married couples how they met. It's always interesting to hear how two lives became intertwined, how of the nearly infinite number of possible conjunctions this or that one came into being, to hear the first chapter of a story in progress. As a matrimonial lawyer I deal extensively in endings, so it's a relief, a sort of holiday, to visit the realm of beginnings. And I ask because I've always enjoyed telling my own story – our story, I should say – which I'd always felt was unique.

My name is Donald Prout, rhymes with *trout*. My wife, Cameron, and I were on vacation in the Virgin Islands when we met Jack and Jean Van Heusen. At our tiny, expensive resort we would see them in the dining room and on the beach. Etiquette dictated respect for privacy, but there was a quiet, countervailing camaraderie born of the feeling that one's fellow guests shared a level of good taste and financial standing. And the Van Heusens stood out as the only other young couple.

I'd just won a difficult case, sticking it to a rich husband and coming out with a nice settlement despite considerable evidence that my client had been cheating on him with everything in pants for years. Of course I sympathized with the guy, but he had his own counsel, had many inherited millions left over, and it's my job, after all, to give whoever hires me the best possible counsel. Now I was taking what I thought of as, for lack of a better cliché, a well-earned rest. I'd never done much resting, going straight from Amherst – where I'd worked part-time for my tuition – to Columbia Law, to a big midtown firm, where I'd knocked myself out as an associate for six years.

It's a sad fact that the ability to savor long hours of leisure is a gift some of us have lost, or else never acquired. The first morning, within an hour of waking in paradise, I was restless, watching stalk-eyed land crabs skitter sideways across the sand, unwilling or unable to concentrate on the Updike I'd started on the plane. Lying on the beach in front of our cabana, I noticed the attractive young couple emerging from the water, splashing each other. She was a tall brunette with the boyish body of a runway model. Sandy-haired and lanky, he looked like a boy who'd taken a semester off from prep school to go sailing. Over the next few days I couldn't help observing them. They were very affectionate, which seemed to indicate a relatively new marriage (both wore wedding bands). And they had an aura of entitlement, of being very much at home and at ease on this very pricey patch of white sand, so I assumed they came from money. Also they seemed indifferent to the rest of us, unlike those couples who, after a few days of sun and sand in the company of the beloved, invite their neighbors for a daiquiri on the balcony to grope for mutual acquaintances and interests

– anything to be spared the frightening monotony of each other.

In fact I was feeling a little dissatisfied after several days, my wife and I having, more rapidly than I would have thought, exhausted our meager store of observations about the monotonously glorious weather and the subjects which we imagined we never had enough time to discuss at home what with business and the social schedule. And after a relatively satisfying first night, our lovemaking was not as inspired as I had hoped it was going to be. I wanted to leave all the bullshit at home, rejuvenate our marriage and our sex life, tell Cameron my fantasies, pathetically simple and requitable as they were. Yet I found myself unable to broach this topic, stuck as I was in a four-year rut of communicating less and less directly, reluctant for some reason to execute the romantic flourishes – candlelight and flower petals in the bath water and such – she considered so inspiring. And seeing her in her two-piece, I honestly felt that Cameron needed to do a bit of toning and cut back on the sweets.

But the example of the Van Heusens was invigorating. After all, I reasoned, we were also an attractive young couple – an extra pound or two notwithstanding. I thought more highly of us for our ostensible resemblance to them and when I overheard him tell an old gent that he'd recently passed the bar I felt a rush of kinship and self-esteem, since I'd recently made partner at one of the most distinguished firms in New York.

On the evening of our fifth day we struck up a conversation at the poolside bar. I heard them speculating about a yacht out in the bay and told them whom it belonged to, having been told myself when I'd seen it in Tortola a few days earlier. I half expected him to recognize the name, to claim friendship with the owners, but he only said, 'Oh, really? Nice boat.'

The sun was melting into the ocean, dyeing the water red and pink and gold. We all sat, hushed, watching the spectacle. I reluctantly broke the silence to remind the waiter that I had specified a piña colada on the rocks, not frozen, my teeth being sensitive to crushed ice. Within minutes the sun had slipped out of sight, sending up a last flare, and then we began to chat. Eventually they told us they lived in one of those eminently respectable communities on the North Shore of Boston.

They asked if we had kids, and we said no, not yet. When I said, 'You?' Jean blushed and referred the question to her husband.

After a silent exchange he turned to us and said, 'Jeannie's pregnant.'

'We haven't really told anyone yet,' she added.

Cameron beamed at Jean and smiled encouragingly in my direction. We had been discussing this very topic lately. She was ready; I didn't feel quite so certain myself. Still, I think we both were pleased to be the recipients of this confidence, even though it was a function of our very lack of real intimacy, and of the place and time, for we learned, somewhat sadly, that this was their last night.

When I mentioned my profession, Jack solicited my advice; he would start applying to firms when they returned home. I was curious, of course, how he had come to the law so relatively late – he had just referred in passing to his recent thirtieth birthday celebration – and what he'd done with his twenties, but thought it would be indiscreet to ask.

We ordered a second round of drinks and talked until it was fully dark. 'Why don't you join us for dinner?' he said as we all stood on the veranda, hesitant about going our separate ways. And so we did. I was grateful for the company, and Cameron seemed to be enlivened by the break in routine. I found Jean increasingly attractive – confident and funny – while her husband was wry and self-deprecating in a manner which suited a young man who was probably a little too rich and happy for anyone else's good. He seemed to be keeping his lights on dim.

As the dinner plates were cleared away, I said, 'So tell me, how did you two meet?'

Cameron laughed at the introduction of my favorite parlor game. Jack and Jean exchanged a long look, seeming to consult about whether to reveal their great secret. He laughed through his nose, and then she began to laugh; within moments they were both in a state of high hilarity. To be sure, we'd had several drinks and two bottles of wine with dinner, and excepting Jean, none of us was legally sober. Cameron in particular seemed to me to be getting a little sloppy, particularly in contrast to the abstinent Jean; when she reached again for the wine bottle I tried to catch her eye, but she was bestowing her bright, blurred attention on our companions. 'How we met,' Jack said to his wife. 'God. You want to tackle this one?'

She shook her head. 'I think you'd better.'

'Cigar?' he asked, producing two metal tubes from his pocket. Though I've resisted the cigar fetish indulged in by so many of my colleagues, I occasionally smoke one with a client or an associate, and I took one now. He handed me a cutter and lit us up, then leaned back and stroked his sandy bangs away from his eyes and released a spume of smoke.

'Maybe it's not such an unusual story,' he proposed.

Jean laughed skeptically.

'You sure you don't mind, honey?' he asked.

She considered, shrugged her shoulders, then shook her head. 'It's up to you.'

'Well, I think this story begins when I got thrown out of Bowdoin,' he said. 'Not to put too fine a point on it, I was dealing pot. Well, pot and a little coke, actually.' He stopped to check our reaction.

I, for one, tried to keep an open, inviting demeanor, eager for him to continue. I won't say I was shocked, though I was certainly surprised.

'I got caught.' He smiled. 'By agreeing to pack up my old kit bag and go away forever I escaped prosecution. My parents were none too pleased about the whole thing, but unfortunately for them, virtually that week I'd come into a little bit of Gramps's filthy lucre and there wasn't much they could do about it. I was tired of school anyway. It's funny, I enjoyed it when I finally went back a few years ago to get my BA and then law school, but at the time it was wasted on me. Or I was wasted on it. Wasted in general. I'd wake up in the morning and fire up the old bong and then huff up a few lines to get through geology seminar.'

He pulled on his stogie, shaking his head ruefully at the memory of his youthful excess. He didn't seem particularly ashamed as much as bemused, as if he were describing the behavior of an incorrigible cousin.

'Well, I went sailing for about a year – spent some time in these waters, actually, some of the best sailing waters in the world – and then drifted back to Boston. I'd run through most of my capital, but I didn't feel ready to hit the books again and somehow I just kind of naturally got back in touch with my suppliers from Bowdoin days. I still had a boat, a little thirty-six-footer. And I got back in the trade. It was different then – this was ten years ago, before the Colombians really moved in. Everything was more relaxed. We were gentlemen outlaws, adrenaline junkies, sail bums, freaks with an entrepreneurial streak.'

He frowned slightly, as if hearing the faint note of self-justification, of self-delusion, of sheer datedness. I'd largely avoided the drug culture of the seventies, but even I could remember when drugs were viewed as the sacraments of a vague liberation theology or, later, as a slightly risky form of recreation. But in this era the romance of drug dealing was a hard sell, and Jack seemed to realize it.

'Well, that's how we saw it then,' he amended. 'Let's just say that we were less ruthless and less financially motivated than the people who eventually took over the business.'

Wanting to discourage his sudden attack of scruples, I waved to the waiter for another bottle of wine.

'Make sure it's not too chilled,' Cameron shouted at the retreating waiter. 'My husband has very sensitive teeth.' I suppose she thought this was quite funny.

'Anyway, I did quite well,' Jack continued. 'Initially I was very hands-on, rendezvousing with mother ships out in the water beyond Nantucket, hauling small loads in a hollow keel. Eventually my partner and I moved up the food chain. We were making money so fast we had a hard time thinking of ways to launder it. I mean, you can't just keep hiding it under your mattress. First we were buying cars and boats in cash and then we bought a bar in Cambridge to run some of the profits through. We were actually paying taxes on drug money just so we could show some legitimate income. We always used to say we'd get out before it got too crazy, once we'd really put aside a big stash, but there was so much more cash to be made, and craziness is like anything else, you get into it one step at a time and no single step really feels like it's taking you over the cliff. Until you go right over the edge and then it's too late. You're smoking reefer in high school and then doing lines and all of a sudden you're buying AK-forty-sevens and bringing hundred-kilo loads into Boston Harbor.'

I wasn't about to point out that some of us never even thought of dealing drugs, let alone buying firearms. I refilled his wineglass, nicely concealing my skepticism, secretly pleased to hear this golden boy revealing his baser metal. But I have to say I was intrigued.

'This goes on for two, three years. I wish I could say it wasn't fun, but it was. The danger, the secrecy, the money . . .' He pulled on his cigar and looked out over the water. 'So anyway, we set up one of our biggest deals ever, and our buyer's been turned. Facing fifteen to life on his own, so he delivers us up on a platter. A *very* exciting moment. We're in a warehouse in Back Bay and suddenly twenty narcs are pointing thirty-eights at us.'

'And one of them was Jean,' Cameron proposed.

I shot her a look, but she was gazing expectantly at her counterpart.

'For the sake of our new friends here,' Jean said, 'I wish I had been.' She looked at her husband and touched his wrist and at that moment I found her extraordinarily desirable. 'I think you're boring these nice people.'

'Not at all,' I protested, directing my reassurance at the story-teller's wife. I was genuinely sorry for her sake that she was party to this sordid tale. She turned and smiled at me, as I'd hoped she would, and for a moment I forgot about the story altogether as I conjured up a sudden vision: slipping from the cabana for a walk later that night, unable to sleep . . . and encountering her out at the edge of the beach, talking, both claiming insomnia, then confessing that we'd been thinking of each other, a long kiss and a slow recline to the soft sand . . .

'You must think – ' She smiled helplessly. 'Well, I don't know what you must think. Jack's never really told anyone about all of this before. You're probably shocked.'

'Please, go on,' said Cameron. 'We're dying to hear the rest. Aren't we, Don?'

I nodded, a little annoyed at this aggressive use of the marital pronoun. Her voice seemed loud and grating, and the gaudy print blouse I've always hated seemed all the more garish beside Jeannie's elegant but sexy navy halter.

'Long story short,' said Jack, 'I hire Carson Baxter to defend me. And piece by piece he gets virtually every shred of evidence thrown out. Makes it disappear right before the jury's eyes. Then he sneers at the rest. I mean, the man's the greatest performer I've ever seen – '

'He's brilliant,' I murmured. Baxter was one of the finest defense attorneys in the country. Although I didn't always share his political views, I admired his adherence to his

151

principles and his legal scholarship. Actually he was kind of a hero to me. I don't know why, but I was surprised to hear his name in this context.

'So I walked,' Jack concluded.

'You were acquitted?' I asked.

'Absolutely.' He puffed contentedly on his cigar. 'Of course, you'd think that would be the end of the story and the end of my illicit but highly profitable career. Alas, unfortunately not. Naturally, I told myself and everyone else I was going straight. But after six months the memory of prison and the bust had faded, and a golden opportunity practically fell into my lap, a chance for one last big score. The retirement run. The one you should never make. Always a mistake, these farewell gigs.' He laughed.

'That waiter's asleep on his feet,' Jean said. 'Like the waiter in that Hemingway story. He's silently jinxing you, Jack Van Heusen, with a special voodoo curse for long-winded white boys, because he wants to reset the table and go back to the cute little turquoise-and-pink staff quarters and make love to his wife the chubby laundress who is waiting for him all naked on her fresh white linen.'

'I wonder how the waiter and the laundress met,' Jack said cheerfully, standing up and stretching. 'That's probably the best story.'

My beloved wife said, 'Probably they met after Don yelled at her about a stain on his linen shirt and the waiter comforted her.'

Jack looked at his watch. 'Good God, ten-thirty already, way past official Virgin Islands bedtime.'

'But you can't go to bed yet,' Cameron said. 'You haven't even met your wife.'

152

'Oh, right. So anyway, a while later I met Jean and we fell in love and got married and lived happily ever after.'

'No fair,' Cameron shrieked.

'I'd be curious to hear your observations about Baxter,' I said quietly.

'The hell with Baxter,' Cameron said. When she was drinking, her voice took on a more pronounced nasal quality as it rose in volume. 'I want to hear the love story.'

'Let's at least take a walk on the beach,' Jean suggested, standing up.

So we rolled out to the sand and dawdled along the water's edge as Jack resumed the tale.

'Well, my partner and I went down to the Keys and picked up a boat, a Hatteras Sixty-two with a false bottom. Had a kid in the Coast Guard on our payroll and another in customs and they were going to talk us through the coastal net on our return. For show we load up the boat with a lot of big-game fishing gear, these huge Nakamichi rods and reels. And we stow the real payload – the automatic weapons with nightscopes and the cash. The guns were part of the deal, thirty of them, enough for a small army. The Colombians were always looking for armament, and we picked these up cheap from an Israeli who had to leave Miami real quick. It was a night like this, a warm winter starry Caribbean night, when the rudder broke about a hundred miles off Cuba. We started to drift, and by morning we got reeled in by a Cuban naval vessel. Well, you can imagine how they reacted when they found the guns and the cash. I mean, think about it, an American boat loaded with guns and cash and high-grade electronics. We tried to explain that we were just drug dealers, but they weren't buying it.'

We had come to the edge of the beach; farther on, a rocky ledge rose up from the gently lapping water of the cove. Jack knelt down and scooped up a handful of fine silvery sand. Cameron sat down beside him. I remained standing, looking up at the powdery spray of stars above us, feeling in my intoxicated state that I was exercising some important measure of autonomy by refusing to sit just because Jack was sitting. By this time I simply did not approve of Jack Van Heusen nor of the fact that this self-confessed drug runner was about to enter the practice of law. And I suppose I didn't sanction his happiness either – with his obvious wealth, whether inherited or illicit, and his beautiful and charming wife.

'That was the worst time of my life,' he said softly, the jauntiness receding. Jean, who had been standing beside him, knelt down and put a hand on his shoulder. Suddenly he smiled and patted her arm. 'But hey – at least I learned Spanish, right?'

Cameron chuckled appreciatively.

'After six months in a Cuban prison, my partner, the captain and I were sentenced to death as American spies. They'd kept us apart the whole time, hoping to break us. And they would've, except that we couldn't tell them what they wanted to hear because we were just a couple of dumb drug runners and not CIA.'

I sat down on the sand, finally, drawing my knees up against my chest, watching Jean's sympathetic face as if her husband's tawdry ordeal, reflected there, would become more compelling. I couldn't feel very sorry for him – he'd gotten himself into this mess. But I could see she knew at least some of the ghastly details that he was eliding for us, and that it pained her. And for that, I felt sorry for her.

'Anyway, we were treated better than most of the Cuban dissidents because they always had to consider the possibility of using us for barter or propaganda. A few weeks before we're supposed to be shot, I manage to get a message to Baxter, who flies down to Havana and uses his leftist cred to get an audience with fucking Fidel. This is when it's illegal to even *go* to Cuba. And Baxter has his files with him, and – here's the beauty part – he uses the same evidence he discredited in Boston to convince Castro and his defense ministry that we're honest to God drug dealers as opposed to dirty Yankee spies. And they release us into Baxter's custody. But when we fly back to Miami' – he paused, looked around at his audience – 'the Feds are waiting for us on the tarmac. A welcoming committee of G-men standing there sweating in their cheap suits. They arrest all four of us for violating the embargo by coming from Cuba. Of course, the Feds know the real story – they've been monitoring this for the better part of a year. Out of the fucking *fritada* pan – '

'The *sartén*, actually,' Jean corrected impishly.

'Yeah, yeah.' He stuck his tongue out at her, then resumed. 'I thought I was going to lose it right there on the runway. After almost seven months in a cell without a window, thinking I was free and then – '

'God,' Cameron blurted, 'you must have been – '

'I was. So now the FBI contacts Havana to ask for the evidence which led to our acquittal as spies so that they can use it to bust us for a smuggling rap.'

I heard the sounds of a thousand insects and the lapping of water as he paused and smiled.

'And the Cubans say, basically – *Fuck you, Yankee pigs*. And we all walk. And Lord, it was sweet.'

To my amazement, Cameron began to applaud. She was, I now realized, thoroughly drunk.

'We still haven't heard about Jean,' I noted. As if I suspected, and was about to prove, Your Honor, that in point of fact they had never actually met at all.

Jean shared with her husband a conspiratorial smile that deflated me. Turning to me, she said, 'My name is Jean Baxter Van Heusen.'

I'm not a complete idiot. 'Carson Baxter's daughter,' I said, and she nodded.

Cameron broke out laughing. 'That's just great, I love it.'

'How did your father feel about it?' I said, sensing a weak point.

Jean's smile disappeared. She picked up a handful of sand and let it slip through her fingers. 'Not too good. Apparently it's one thing to defend a drug dealer, prove his innocence and take his money. But it's quite another thing when he falls in love with your precious daughter.'

'Jeannie used to come to my trial to watch her father perform. And that, to answer your question, finally, is how we met. In court. Exchanging steamy looks, then steamy notes, across a stuffy courtroom.' Pulling her close against his shoulder he added, 'God, you looked good.'

'Right,' she said. 'Anything without a Y chromosome would've looked good to you after three months in custody.'

'After I was acquitted we started seeing each other secretly. Carson didn't know when he flew to Cuba. He didn't have a clue until we walked out of the courthouse in Miami and Jean threw her arms around me. And except for a few scream-and-threat fests, he hasn't really spoken to us since that day.' He paused. 'He did send me a bill, though.'

'The really funny thing,' Jean said, 'is that Jack was so impressed with my dad that he decided to go to law school.'

Cameron laughed again. At least one of us found this funny. My response took me a long time to sort out. As a student of the law you learn to separate emotion from facts, but in this case I suffered a purely emotional reaction. I cannot justify in rational terms. Unfairly, perhaps, I felt disillusioned with the great Carson Baxter. And I felt personally diminished, robbed of the pride I'd felt in discussing my noble profession with an acolyte only a few hours before, and cheated out of the righteous condescension I had felt only minutes before.

'What a great story,' Cameron said.

'So what about you guys,' said Jean, sitting on the moonlit sand with her arm around her husband. 'What's your wildly romantic story? Tell us about how you two met.'

Cameron turned to me eagerly, smiling with anticipation. 'Tell them, Don.'

I stared out into the bay at a light on the yacht we'd all admired earlier, and I thought about the boy who'd been polishing brass on deck when we walked up the dock on Tortola, a shirtless teenager with limp white hair hanging on his coppery shoulders, bobbing his head and humming, looking forward, I imagined, to a night on the town.

I turned back to my wife, grinning beside me in the cold sand. 'You tell them,' I said.

THE QUEEN AND I

AS THE TIRED LIGHT drains into the western suburbs beyond the river, the rotting pier at the end of Gansevoort Street begins to shudder and groan with life. From inside a tin-roofed warehouse, human beings stagger out into the steamy dusk like bats leaving their cave. Inside the shed, one can make out in the dimness a sprawling white mountain, the slopes of which are patched with sleeping bags, mattresses, blankets, cardboard and rafts of plywood. An implausible rumor circulates among the inhabitants of this place that the white mesa is made of salt which was once, when there were still funds for municipal services, spread on the icy city streets in winter; at present the rusting warehouse serves as a huge dormitory and rat ranch. At dusk the inmates rise to work, crawling out into the last light to dress and put on their makeup. Down on the edge of the highway along the foot of the pier, the shiny cars of pimps and johns wait alongside the beat-up vans from the rescue missions and religious organizations, ready to compete for the bodies and souls of the pier-dwellers.

I watch as three queens share a mirror and a lip-stick, blinking in the slanted light. One of them steps away a few feet, creating a symbolic privacy in which to pull up his skirt demurely and take a torrential leak. A second lights up a cigarette and tugs on a pair of fishnet hose. The third is my friend Marilyn, queen of Little West Twelfth Street. It's my first night on the job.

I ran into Marilyn in the emergency room at St Vincent's a couple days before. I went in for gingivitis, my gums bleeding and disappearing up the sides of my teeth from bad nutrition and bad drugs. It's a common street afflic-tion, another credential in my downward slide toward authenticity. Marilyn had a broken nose, three cracked ribs and assorted bruises from a trick tormented by second thoughts.

'I thought you had a pimp, Marilyn,' I said, watching a gunshot victim bleeding freely on a gurney.

'The pimp, he get killed by the Colombians,' said Marilyn. 'He never protect me anyways, the bastard. He punch me hisself.' Marilyn laughed through his nose, then winced. When he could speak again he said, 'Last time my nose got broke it's my papa do the breaking. He beat the shit out me when he find me dressed in Mama's wedding gown. I'm holding the lipstick and he opens the door of my room. Smack me good, scream at me, call me a dirty little *maricón*, he don't want no *maricón* for a son. The boy last night, he was like that, this big bulging muscle New Chursey boy. After I do him, he start hitting, calling me faggot. A lot them like that, they don't like what they want. Hey, man,' he said, scrutinizing me with new interest. 'Why don't you be my pimp? I give you five dollar every trick.'

It was a measure of my prospects that I thought this was a pretty good offer. In fact, I'd been unemployed by another Colombian murder and was sleeping in Abingdon Square Park. I was dealing halves and quarters of coke out of a bar on Thirteenth when my man got whacked and I was left without a connection. Before that I'd been in a band, but the drummer OD'd, and the bassist moved to LA.

When I first met Marilyn I was living in a cellar in the Meat District. Marilyn worked all night, and I was up jonesing on coke or crack and trying to write. I'm a songwriter, you see, a poet. There is beautiful, ugly music inside me, which plays in the performance space deep in my mind. Walking the streets, doing the bars, I hear snatches of it in the distance, above the subliminal bass line of the urban heartbeat. I am most attuned to it in moments of transport, when I'm loaded on cheap wine or crack. Sometimes I'm dead certain that with one more drink, one more hit, I'll grasp its essence and carry it back with me to the other side. An aesthetician of ugliness, I am living here in the gutter like Prince Hal, biding my time, waiting to burst forth like a goddamn sun.

A refugee from the western suburbs, I used to skip school and take the bus into the city. I hung out on St Mark's Place and the Bowery, copping the look and the attitude of punk, discovering Bukowski and the Beats in the bookshops. Returning to the subdivisions of Jersey was an embarrassment. The soil was too thin for art. No poetry could ever grow in the grapefruit rinds of the compost heap. Ashamed of my origins, neither high nor low, I dreamed of smoky bars and cafés, steaming slums. I believed that the down and dirty would lead me to the height of consciousness, that to conceive beauty it was necessary to sleep with ugliness. I've been in that bed for several years now. So far nobody's knocked up.

Like Dylan says, *Someday everything is gonna be different, / When I paint my masterpiece.* I'll be rich and famous, photographed with models who will suddenly find me incredibly attractive – my goodness, where have I been all their short naughty long-legged lives? – and I will do a lot of expensive designer drugs and behave very badly and ruin my promising career and end up right back here in the gutter. And I'll write a song cycle about it. It'll be excellently poignant, even tragic.

Marilyn grew up in Spanish Harlem, where he was christened Jesús, a delicate boy with a sweet face who is a plausible piece of ass as a girl. He wants to get married and live the kind of life I grew up in. Except he wants to do it as a woman. At night he looks longingly out over the Hudson at the dim glow of suburban Jersey the way I used to look over from the other side at the lights of Manhattan. He wants a three-bedroom house he can clean and polish while awaiting a husband who works in the city. There's a huge Maxwell House sign across the river from the Gansevoort pier, and he told me once that when he wakes up at the end of the average American workday he remembers the tuneful Maxwell House commercials he saw as a kid, dreaming about percolating a pot of coffee for a sleepy hubby.

The doctor who gives Marilyn his hormone shots says

that more than half the – what shall we call them? – the people who get the operation get married, and that more than half of those don't tell their husbands about their former lives as men. I personally find this just a teensy bit hard to believe. But Marilyn doesn't, and he's saving up for the operation.

Poor Marilyn with his broken snout. In this business he needs to be able to breathe through his nose. I decide to give it a shot. Could be a song in it. Plus I'm stone broke.

So as the sun goes down beyond the river into the middle of America where the cows are heading back to their barns and guys with lunchboxes and briefcases are dragging ass home to their wives, I'm trudging toward the Meat District with Marilyn, who is wearing fishnet hose under a green vinyl miniskirt and a loose black top. The Queen and I.

'How I look, honey?' Marilyn asks.

'Looking bad, looking good,' I say.

'This my Madonna look. Those Chursey boys – they love it.'

By now I'm sure you've guessed that Marilyn is currently a blonde.

The smell gets worse as we approach Washington and Gansevoort, which is Marilyn's beat – the warehouses full of dead meat, the prevailing smell of rot inextricably linked in my mind with the stench of urine and excrement and spent semen. A sign reads: VEAL SPECIALISTS: HOT HOUSE BABY LAMBS, SUCKLING PIGS & KID GOATS. Whoa! Sounds like that shit should be illegal, know what I'm saying?

With darkness falling, a slow and funky metamorphosis is taking place. Refrigerated trucks haul away from loading docks while rough men in bloody aprons yank down metal shutters and padlock sliding doors. The suffocating smell of rotting meat hangs over the neighborhood and, when the breeze blows east off the Hudson, infiltrates the smug apartments and cafés of Greenwich Village – which is the only good thing I can say about this stench.

As the trucks disappear toward New Jersey and upstate, strange creatures materialize on the broken sidewalks as if spontaneously generated from the rotting flesh. Poised on high heels, undulant with the exaggerated shimmy of courtship – a race of lanky stylized bipeds commands the street corners. They thrust lips and hips at any cars that pass this time of night, the area not exactly being on the direct route to anywhere except hell or Hoboken. Motorists that find their way here cruise slowly down the unlit, cobbled streets, circling and returning to scout the sidewalk sirens. Sometimes a car slows to a stop near one of the posing figures, who then leans toward the driver's window to consult, haggle and flirt, sometimes to walk around the car and slip in the passenger door, reappearing a few minutes later.

The 'girls' of Washington Street come in all sizes, colors and nose shapes; and in this light not all of them are hard to look at. One lifts a halter top to expose a pair of taut white breasts as a red Toyota with Connecticut plates crawls past. It's just barely conceivable that some of these sports who transact for five minutes of sex believe they're getting it straight. But ladies, I wouldn't count on it. I mean if your fiancé gets busted down here you might think about canceling the band and the tent and the cake. Or maybe not. They're probably good family men, most of them.

And so long as clothes and makeup stay in place, no one needs to start parsing his proclivities. Sometimes the cops sweep through to meet arrest quotas; johns who find their pleasure interrupted by a sudden, official rap on the window almost always act shocked when the cops expose the gender of their sexual partners with a playful tug of the waistband or the not-so-playful rending of a skirt.

The clientele is nothing if not diverse, arriving in limos and Chevies, Jags and Toyotas. Whenever a certain homophobic movie star is visiting New York – a comic renowned for obscene stand-up routines which outrage the gay and feminist communities – his white stretch limousine is bound to linger on Washington Street in the small hours of the morning.

I take up a post beneath a sagging metal awning, half concealed in the shadows, while Marilyn takes out his compact to check on the goods. He frowns. 'That salt is terrible for my skin. Suck the moisture right out, sleeping every night on a big pile of salt. Even the rats don't like living on the salt.' Is that because the rats are worried about their complexions? I wonder. Meantime, near the curb, Marilyn strikes a pose he has borrowed from a Madonna video. Just up the street is Randi, who claims he used to play with the Harlem Globetrotters. Wearing a leather mini and a red halter, Randi stands six foot eight in heels beneath a sign that reads FRANKS SALAMI BOLOGNA LIVERWURST KNOCKWURST STEW MEATS & SKIRT STEAKS. Truth in advertising.

Down Gansevoort, at the edge of the district, the neon sign of a fashionable diner emits a pink glow. So very far away – this place where the assholes I went to college with are tossing back colored drinks and discussing the stock market and interoffice gropings. Like my former best friend George Bing, who wanted to be a poet and works for an ad agency in midtown. We roomed together at NYU, which I dropped out of after two years because I was way too cool. After George graduated we'd meet for drinks at the Lion's Head or the Whitehorse, where he thought he was slumming and I felt like an interloper among the gentry. So excited when he first walked in as a freshman – with a fake ID from a store on Forty-second Street – that Dylan Thomas had died practically where we were sitting, but gradually, over the years, he decided that the Welsh bard had wasted and abused his talent. I mean, sure, George admitted, he was great, but what was so bad about being comfortable, taking care of your health, eating sensibly and writing copy for Procter and Gamble in between cranking out those lyrical heart's cries? And I'm on my best behavior, nodding like an idiot coming down off something I smoked or snorted and hoping the bartender won't remember he threw me out three months before. And eventually, I think it became too embarrassing for both of us. I stopped calling, and Lord knows I don't have a phone, except maybe the open-air unit on the corner of Hudson and Twelfth. Actually, it's been a relief to quit pretending.

Farther down Washington Street a trio of junkies builds a fire in a garbage can, although the night is hot and steamy – the heat of the day, stored up in the concrete and asphalt, coming off now, cooking everyone slowly like so much meat. These old guys, after they've been on the street a few years they never really get warm again. The winter cold stays in your bones through the long stinking summer and forever, like a scar. The old farts wear overcoats and boots in August. That way you don't have to change clothes for winter. One style fits all.

I'm just fine in my black T-shirt and denim jacket, which doubles as a blanket, thanks. Be off the street before that happens to me. When I paint my masterpiece. Franks salami bologna.

A red Nissan slows to a stop. Marilyn sashays over to the car and schmoozes the driver, turns and waves to me. I come out of the shadow to reveal myself in all my freaky emaciated menace, moonwhite face and dyed black hair, my yellow teeth in their bleedy gums. Marilyn zips around to the passenger side and climbs into the car, which makes a right and slows to a stop a half block down the street, where I can still see it. Farther on, a bum in an overcoat parks his overflowing shopping cart on the sidewalk and peers in the window at the brightly lit diners eating steak *frites*.

Eventually Marilyn comes back from his date, adjusting his clothes and checking his makeup in a compact, like a model. That's what he calls it – a date. He hands me a damp, crumpled fiver. I don't want to think about the dampness at all. I want to scrape the bill off my palm and throw it into the stinking street, but Marilyn's all excited about being back at work and planning for the future. He's talking about how it will be after the operation, when he gets married and moves to New Chursey. I want to slap him and make him understand that it's the land of the living dead. It's not real, like this fabulous life we're living here on Gansevoort Street. The flesh they grill on their Webers out in Morristown comes out of the very warehouses against which we bravely slouch.

At least Marilyn will be spared the ordeal of having a rotten suburban brat who will grow up to resent and despise him for being a boring submissive housewife.

As the night deepens, business picks up, and I nearly become accustomed to the layered stench, the several octaves of decay. The old men sharing a bottle around the fire pass out and the fire dies. I skulk over to Hudson and buy myself a bottle of blackberry brandy to keep my motor running. A dealer strolls by offering coke, crack and smoke. At first I think, No, I'm on duty, but the second time he comes by I have twenty dollars in my pocket from Marilyn, and I buy a little rock and fire it up, tickling my brain, making me feel righteous and empowered – I'm here, I'm cool, I'm feeling so good, I'm back on my feet and the future is mine, if I can just smoke a little more of this I'll keep from slipping back, just a little more to maintain, to stop this fading, this falling away from the perfect moment that was here just a minute ago, to hear that perfect tune in my deep brain, that masterpiece.

Franks bologna et cetera.

The buzz has slipped away like a heartbreakingly hot girl at a bar who said she'd be back in a minute, promise. Leaving me oh so very sad and cranky. Where is the goddamn dealer?

The traffic in and out of the diner picks up around four when the clubs close, yellow cabs pulling up to dispense black-clad party people like Pez, the hip boys and girls who are not yet ready for bed. I buy a so-called quarter of alleged toot and snort it all at once thinking it will carry me farther, slower than smoking rocks.

Marilyn gets eleven dates for the night, a cavalcade of perverts representing several states, classes and ethnic groups, including a Hasidic jeweler with long Slinky sidelocks that bounce up and down as he bucks to fulfillment in the front seat of his black Lincoln, a construction worker with Jersey plates in a Subaru still wearing his hard hat and a stretch limo where the guy tells Marilyn he's in the movie business and tips twenty.

The Lambs of God van cruises up, pulls over beside us. The priest says, 'Top of the morning, Marilyn.' He looks surprised, not necessarily happy, when I slink out of my vampire shadow.

'Hello, Father,' says Marilyn. 'You looking for some fun tonight?'

'No, no, just checking to see that you're not . . . needing anything.'

'Fine thanks, Father. And you?'

'Bless you and be careful, my child.' The priest guns the engine and pulls away.

'Very nice, the father, but shy,' says Marilyn, a note of disappointment in his voice. 'I think maybe you scare him off.'

'The shy shepherd,' I say.

'I stay at that Lambs of God shelter one night and he didn't ask me for nothing,' says Marilyn, as if describing a heroic feat of selfless ministry. 'That day he just cop a little squeeze when I'm leaving. Food pretty decent, too.' We watch a car go by, slowly, the driver looking us over from behind his sunglasses. He seemed about to stop, then peeled out and tore down the street. After a long pause Marilyn said, 'My very first date was a priest, when I was an altar boy. He give me some wine.'

'Sounds very romantic,' I say, recalling my own altar boyhood in another life. In awe of my proximity to the sacred rituals, I didn't smoke or swear and I confessed my impure thoughts to the eager priest behind the screen until my thoughts transmuted themselves to deeds on Mary Lynch's couch one afternoon, which I failed to mention at my next confession, suffering the guilt of the damned as I slunk away from the confessional booth. When lightning failed to strike me through the days and weeks that followed, I began to resent my guilt and then the faith that was so at odds with my secret nature and, finally, to exult in my rebellion. And as I turned away from my parents and Church, I created my own taboo-venerating cult. Which perverse faith I am stubbornly observing here at five in the morning at the corner of Gansevoort and Washington.

Another car cruises by slowly, a junkyard Buick with two guys in the front seat. Twos are potentially dangerous, so I decide I'll show my flag and talk to them myself. I tell Marilyn to stay put, then I saunter over to the car. The driver has to open the door because the window won't roll down. Two small Hispanics in their fifties. 'Twenty-five apiece,' I say, nodding toward Marilyn. 'And you stay on this block.' Finally we agree on thirty-five for two.

I wave Marilyn over and he climbs in the back seat, and I'm just leaning back against the building lighting a smoke when Marilyn comes howling and tumbling out of the car, crawling furiously as the car peels out, tires squealing on the cobblestones. Marilyn flings himself on me and I hold him as he sobs. *'Es mi padre,'* he wails. *'Mi padre.'*

'A priest?' I say, hopefully.

He shakes his head violently against my shoulder and suddenly raises his face and starts apologizing for getting makeup on me, wiping at my jacket, still crying. 'I ruin your jacket,' he says, crying hysterically. It's all I can do to convince him that I don't give a shit about the jacket, which started out filthy anyway.

'Are you sure it was . . . him?' I say.

Gulping air, he nods vehemently. 'It's the first time I see him in three years,' Marilyn says. He's sobbing and shaking, and I'm more than a little freaked out myself. I mean, Jesus.

Finally, when he calms down, I suggest we call it a night. I make him drink the rest of the blackberry brandy and walk him back to the dock in the grainy gray light. As the sun comes up behind us, we stand on the edge of the pier and look out over the river at the Maxwell House sign. I can't think of anything to say. I put my arm around him and he sniffles on my shoulder. From a distance we would look like any other couple, I think. Finally I suggest he get some sleep, and he picks his way across the rotting boards back to the salt mountain. And that's the end of my career as a pimp.

A year after this happened, I went back to look for Marilyn. Most of the girls on the street were new to me, but I found Randi, the former Globetrotter, who at first didn't

173

remember me. I do look different now. He thought I was a cop, and then guessed I was a reporter. He wanted money to talk, so I finally gave him ten, and he said, 'I know you, you was that crackhead.' Nice to be remembered. I asked if he'd seen Marilyn and he said Marilyn had disappeared suddenly – 'Maybe like, I don't know, seems like a year ago.' He couldn't tell me anything else and he didn't want to know.

About a year after that I spotted a wedding announcement in the *Times*. I admit I'd been checking all that time – perusing what we once called the women's sports pages – like an idiot, occasionally rewarded with the picture of a high school or college acquaintance, and then one fine morning I saw a picture that stopped me. Actually, I think I noticed the name first – otherwise I might not have stopped at the picture. MARILYN BERGDORF TO WED RONALD DUBOWSKI. It would be just like Marilyn to name himself after a chic department store. I stared at the photo for a long time, and though I wouldn't swear to it in a murder trial, I think it was my Marilyn – surgically altered, one presumes – that married Ronald Dubowski, orthodontist, of Oyster Bay, Long Island. I suppose I could have called, but I didn't.

So I don't really know how that night affected Marilyn, if it changed his life, if he is now officially and anatomically a woman, or even if he's alive. I do know that lives can change overnight, though it usually takes much longer than that to comprehend what has happened, to sense that we have changed direction. A week after Marilyn almost had sex with his father, I checked myself into Phoenix House. I called my parents for the first time in more than a year. Now, two years later, I have a boring job and a crummy apartment and a girlfriend who makes the rest of it seem almost okay. I'd be lying if I said there weren't times I miss the old days, or that I don't breathe a huge sigh of relief when I climb on the train after a few hours spent visiting my parents, or that it's a gas being straight all the time, but still I'm grateful.

You think you're living a secret and temporary life, underground, in the dark. You don't imagine that some-one will drive up the street or walk in the door or look through the window – someone who will reveal you to yourself not as you hope to be in some glorious future metamorphosis but as you find yourself at that moment. Whatever you are doing then, you will have to stop and say, 'Yes, this is me.'

REUNION

THE EARLY MORNING SILENCE of the graveyard is broken by the approach of a car. I duck behind a stone as the sound of the engine rises toward the gate and falls away among the streets of the town. Sitting on a flat marble slab, Tory continues cutting pieces of masking tape, which she attaches to the back of her hand. The cemetery grass is brown and worn, as if it has been grazed by sheep. The last shreds of morning haze cling to the old stones, which tilt at eccentric angles.

I stand up again but remain hunched, feeling conspicuous among the squat headstones, while Tory seems right at home, though she has warned me this is illegal. The old cemetery is surrounded by the town; although it is wooded and occupies a rise, I feel exposed. A seagull cruises overhead with an inquisitive squawk. My eyes are dry and itchy from waking too early.

'Stretch this as tight as you can across the face of the stone,' Tory says, holding out a big sheet of newsprint from the tablet we picked up at a hobby store last night. I kneel as Tory directs me to raise and lower the paper until finally it's just where she wants it, and she secures it with masking tape. Then she rubs the crayon across the paper. Crayons, drawing tablets, masking tape. I find it strange that we have come to visit the dead with children's art supplies. 'Not too hard,' she says. White, archaic letters rise to the surface of the paper. The letters gradually become words. HERE emerges, then BODY OF. I think of it as ghost writing. The inscription states the facts: name, age and parents. The stone is a triptych, the outer tablets bearing images of a grinning skeleton on one side and Father Time on the other. A skull appears under Tory's crayon, then ribs. 'This guy was very rich,' she says. 'The stonework's amazing. Look at these details – you can even see the anklebones on Father Time.' Tory nods toward the tablet of newsprint. 'Give it a try,' she says.

I stalk the uneven avenues for a likely stone. In the corner near the savings bank I find one dated 1698, with the name NATHANIEL MATHER. A winged skull presides over the inscription AN AGED PERSON WHO HAD SEEN, BUT NINETEEN WINTERS IN THE WORLD. I sit down on the grass and touch the stone. What does it mean? I once read about a disease that accelerates the aging process so rapidly that its victims die of old age in their teens. Or is it just a metaphor? A young man worn down by troubles.

'Michael, come here,' Tory calls.

I get to my feet and look around. 'Where are you?' I ask in a loud whisper.

'Over here.' She raises her hand and waves from behind a cluster of stones. I watch the cemetery gate as another car passes, then scuttle over.

'Look at this.' She points to a lichen-covered stone. The

engraving has a crude, homemade look. THE CHILDREN
OF CHARLES AND SARAH ... The surname is unread-
able. EMILY, TWO YEARS. CHARLES, SEVEN MONTHS.
ETHAN.

'There's no age for Ethan,' I say.

Tory looks up at me. She doesn't say anything at first.
She holds the crayon like a cigarette and touches it to
her lips as she stares at me. Finally she says, 'He died in
childbirth.' She says this as if she holds me responsible.

'Where are the witches,' I ask.

'They didn't bury them in the cemetery. This is hallowed
ground. They put the witches in unmarked graves on
Gallows Hill in Danvers.'

'I wanted to rub a witch's stone.'

'You can do the guy who sentenced them to death. Judge
Hathorne's right over there. That would be a good one for
you to get. A fellow pillar of the legal profession.' Tory is
on her third rubbing of the children's stone. The first two
were black. This one's red. I pick a stone near hers, keeping
an eye on the entrance.

'There was one man named Giles Corry, who refused
to confess or to implicate anyone as a witch, so they put a
beam on his chest and started piling rocks on top to force a
confession. But he refused to speak. They piled more rocks
on. His ribs broke and finally he died.'

'That's a lovely story,' I say.

Tory's a little morbid these days. But she says this grave
rubbing is something she has been doing since she was a
kid. This is the first time we've come up here. Though
we've been living together in New York for over a year,
Tory hasn't been eager to go home for a visit. Her parents

separated shortly before she and I moved into our little apartment. Her mother hung on to the house, but things are strained between her and Tory. I suspect Ginny's unable to live up to the high standards that Tory sets for those she loves, although I'm not sure, because we seldom talk about it. Tory is furious with her father for leaving with another woman; yet she also seems to blame her mother for letting him do so, for not being the kind of woman that no man would ever walk out on.

Shortly after we arrived, Tory gave her mother a lesson in makeup. Ginny submitted patiently as Tory demonstrated the uses of blush and mascara. Ginny has the skin of a tennis player and the hair of a swimmer; the makeup seemed to disappear without a trace moments after it was applied. Later, Tory worked on her mother's taxes; Ginny has an antique shop that was operated for years on the principle of losing money to write off her husband's taxes. But with the division of property hung up in the courts and two years of taxes due on the house, Ginny now is faced with the new and baffling imperative of making money.

The family, sans patriarch, has ostensibly gathered for Bunny's graduation. There are four sisters, spread over ten years, all conspicuously blond. Carol, her new husband, Jim, and her daughter by a former marriage are here from California. Carol's pregnant. Jim's a Christian. Under his tutelage, Carol has been born again. She is the oldest, and according to Tory she has been exemplary, doing all of the stupid and illegal things that her younger sisters might've been tempted to do. Bunny, who just turned twenty-four, is able to seem merely adventurous by comparison. She started Radcliffe but dropped out to marry a cocaine dealer. When the marriage broke up, she moved back in with her parents. In two days she'll graduate from a local state school, where she's dating a married professor twice her age. Tory is the third child. Mary, the youngest, still lives at home and mostly is into cars and boys. I'm not sure whether she likes the boys because they have cars, or the cars because the boys have them. She speaks confidently about horsepower, engine displacement, biceps and pectorals. She doesn't think much of me – I drive a Toyota and wear a thirty-eight regular. Last night at the supper table she noticed me long enough to ask if I would make a lot of money now that I've graduated from law school.

This family reunion might be the last one in the old house. Ginny can't afford to keep it. I'd love to live in a house like this one, an old post-and-beam matchbox core that has been added to in various directions over the last couple hundred years, jammed with primitive furnishings of scarred, fragrant wood; crude iron implements; cloudy bull's-eyed blue-green glass. I like the outbuildings, the sagging, disused stables and greenhouse; even the pool, cracked and covered over with a green scum, has the aspect of an ornamental pond.

I grew up in houses that were vague, standardized descendants of those in this neighborhood. Since arriving yesterday I've conceived an indeterminate fantasy of saving the old homestead with my legal skills, distinctly featuring the gratitude of this family of attractive females.

But for several weeks now I have felt helpless in the face of Tory's medical problems. She has been bleeding erratically. Her gynecologist in New York has several hypotheses. In two days she will check into Mass General for tests, and I'll drive back to New York to start an associateship at Cravath, Swaine & Moore.

On the way home from the cemetery we stop at a package store. Tory waits in the car. A red Camaro is idling in the parking lot, heavy metal blasting from the open windows. Inside the store, a kid with an Iron Maiden T-shirt hefts three cases of beer up to the counter. His denim jacket has the sleeves ripped out, BILLY embroidered above one pocket, HEAVY CHEVY over the other. He asks for three bottles of José Cuervo tequila. The clerk checks his ID doubtfully. 'Frank Sweeney?' he says.

'Yeah, right,' the kid says. The clerk sighs and hands the ID back. Coming out of the store, I spot Mary, Tory's younger sister, inside the Camaro. She waves. The kid with the ID is loading the stuff in the trunk.

'How do you like my wheels?' Mary says. 'Don't tell Mom you saw me, okay? I'm supposed to be at Laura's house.' The kid comes around the side of the car and looks me over. Mary doesn't introduce anyone. They leave in a roar of exhaust.

Back in the car, I describe the scene for Tory, who has been reading. 'She's young,' Tory says. She goes back to her magazine. Mary is the only member of the family who escapes Tory's censure. Tory's still able to see her as the baby. It seems to be something she clings to, this idea that there's still a baby in the family after all that has happened.

In the kitchen, Carol and her daughter, Lily, are playing with Barbies. Carol has four months to go on her next, but she's already huge. Between her religion and her fertility, she's bursting with contentment. Ginny, the aproned matriarch, is fixing lunch. Lily lifts her Barbie toward me and waves it from side to side as she speaks in a high, squeaky voice.

'Look, Barbie, it's Ken.'

'That's not Ken,' Carol says. 'Who is that?'

'That's Michael,' Lily says in her own voice, hiding her face in her mother's arm.

'You like Michael, don't you?' Carol says, doing a Barbie voice.

Lily shakes her head back and forth. She won't look up.

'Don't teach her to be a dumb blonde, Carol,' Tory says.

'And who's that?' Carol says, directing Lily toward Tory.

Tory kneels beside Lily's chair and points her finger at herself. 'Do you remember my name?'

Lily shakes her head and hides it again in her mother's shoulder. She can't remember Tory's name but has the others down cold.

'That's Tory,' Carol says. 'Isn't that a pretty name? *Tory* rhymes with *story* and *glory*, doesn't it?'

Tory says, 'And *gory*.'

'Do we have a kiss for nice Aunt Tory?' Lily shakes her head against her mother's shoulder. Tory stands up and leaves the room.

'Sandwiches are ready,' Ginny says. 'Grilled cheese, tomato and bacon.' Ginny's one of those people who believe that there is very little that can't be fixed by putting a meal on the table.

'Jim doesn't eat bacon,' Carol says.

'I thought he was a Christian. Isn't it Jews who don't eat bacon?'

'We eat low cholesterol.'

Ginny puts the hot tray down on the counter. She takes off the oven mitt and lights a cigarette. 'You eat low cholesterol. You don't smoke. You don't drink. You don't swear, and you don't like it when other people do. Is there anything else I should know as your inn-keeper? Would you maybe like some more hay in your manger?'

'Jesus loves you, Mom.'

Jim, the born-again husband, comes in, looking sleepy. 'Is that bacon I smell?' he says.

'I was going to do fishes and loaves,' Ginny says, 'but I couldn't find a good recipe.'

I find Tory in her room, lying on the bed with a stuffed tiger in her arms.

'I brought you a sandwich,' I say.

She shakes her head. I sit down beside her on the bed. A framed grave rubbing hangs over the headboard. HERE LYES THE BODY OF. The bedside table displays a collection of handmade dolls. I pick up a porcelain doll in peasant costume, then put it back.

'This was my room all the time I was growing up,' Tory says.

'Maybe one of these days we'll buy ourselves a big old house like this,' I suggest. I wish I hadn't said 'maybe,' but I feel uncertain of the future. Tory and I have talked about marriage, though everything seems to be changing. I don't

186

really know what I want. Everything has become so gloomy and difficult lately.

'I don't want a big old house,' Tory says. 'A big old house needs kids in it.'

'Don't be so pessimistic. The doctor said that was a worst-case scenario.'

'Doctors have been treating women like children for centuries.'

There's a knock on the door, and Bunny comes in.

She throws herself down on the bed beside Tory. 'And now the graduate, exhausted from rehearsal in the hot sun, takes a load off her feet,' Bunny says. 'Also, by avoiding her own room, she hopes to escape interrogation at the hands of the mother of the graduate.'

'What interrogation?' Tory says.

'She wants to know whether Bill's going to be at the ceremony.'

'Is he?'

'Of course.'

'You could introduce him as the father of the graduate,' Tory says. 'He's even older than Dad. Is he going to bring his wife with him?'

'He's not older than Dad. They're the same age.'

'That makes it perfect.'

'He's in terrific shape. He works out and plays tennis every day.'

'You're going to ruin the graduation for Mom if she sees him there.'

'She won't see him.'

'Is Dad coming?'

'I didn't invite the bastard.'

The sisters fall silent, both bouncing lightly on the bed, as if responding to some signal I can't hear. The resemblance of the two sisters lying on the bed is eerie and exciting. They seem to lend each other beauty, their juxtaposition creating a context for appreciation. In silence, they exercise a lifetime of intimacy. Outside I hear the clop-clop of a horse on the road. Dust swarms in the wedge of sunshine coming in through the curtains; a shaft of yellow light catches the edge of Bunny's hair and appears to ignite it. Both women have their eyes closed. I watch them. They seem to be asleep.

I go downstairs. Ginny is sitting at the kitchen table, reading a magazine. The TV is on, a game show. Ginny looks up and smiles. 'My *Gourmet* arrived so I'm happy,' she says. 'I hardly ever cook anymore, but I love to read the recipes.' I take a seat at the big round table that is the hub of family activity. The house has dens, living rooms and I'm not sure what else, but everyone hangs out in the kitchen. I wonder if it was always this way.

Ginny closes the magazine and looks up at the television. Then she looks at me. 'Do you think in this day and age it's possible to win an alienation of affection suit?'

'I believe it's very difficult,' I say. 'But I'm afraid it's not my area.' I wish I could tell her something encouraging, save the farm, stay the execution. I imagine myself flat on my back while a hostile jury piles stones on the beam across my chest. I went into law school with a vague notion of righting wrongs. 'I don't know much about divorce law,' I say. 'Corporate marriages are my field. But I could look into it for you.'

'No, that's okay. I've got a lawyer. I shouldn't be bothering you for advice.' She reaches over and pats my hand. 'It's good to have you here. I'm so pleased that Tory has someone like you to take care of her. You're great together.' She lights up a cigarette. 'Carol – I'm just relieved that she's not in jail or the nuthouse. If Jesus is what it takes, fine. Although I must say having those two around makes me want to curse and smoke and drink just out of spite.' She looks at her watch.

'How about a drink, Ginny? I picked up a bottle of vodka.'

'Well, I suppose, since it's the weekend . . .'

'It's an occasion,' I say. 'I think we're well within our rights here.' I fix the drinks. We were pleased to discover, last night, that we both like vodka on the rocks with a splash. Tory was less pleased. She thinks her mother drinks too much.

'I'm so glad you're a sinner,' Ginny says. 'I can't tell you what a relief it is. Carol and Jim were here for two days before you arrived, and it felt like two weeks. Cheers.'

The phone rings. Ginny jumps up and catches it on the second ring. She says hello three times and hangs up. 'That could've been one of three people,' Ginny says after she's back at the table. She raises her hand and holds up a finger. 'It could've been my husband, calling to see if I was out so he could sneak over and steal the silver. He tried one afternoon, but Bunny came home and caught him.' She lifts a second finger. 'It could've been Bill, Bunny's aging lover. He hangs up if I answer because he knows I won't let him talk to Bunny. Can you tell me what a young girl would want with a fifty-five-year-old man? And he's married. He keeps telling her he's going to divorce his wife, but he certainly hasn't told the wife yet. Although she knows all about it.' Ginny raises a third finger. 'Bill's wife is the other mystery-phone-call candidate. She calls sometimes when she doesn't know where her husband is, to see if Bunny's home. She disguises her voice when she asks for Bunny.'

Ginny takes a long sip of her drink. 'You know, I almost feel relieved when I think of Mary drinking beer with boys her own age.'

While I freshen our drinks, Ginny starts dinner. Mary calls to say she's having dinner at Laura's house. I wonder if Ginny knows about Heavy Chevy Billy. I feel uneasy, vaguely responsible for her. What if she's in an accident tonight? Lily cautiously enters the kitchen, without parents, self-conscious and pleased when Ginny and I compliment her on her new dress. She tells us her mommy made it. 'Your *mommy* made it?' Ginny says.

Lily nods.

'Christ really does work miracles,' Ginny says.

Tory comes down. 'Why didn't you wake me up?' she says.

'For what?'

'I don't know. What have you been doing?'

'Saying bad things about you,' Ginny says. 'Want a drink?' I can tell Tory's looking her mother over to see how much she's had.

'I'll have a beer.'

The phone rings again and Ginny grabs it. She says hello several times. Then she says, 'I know it's you,' and hangs up.

'Who?' Tory says.

'I don't know,' Ginny responds.

Supper is chicken Kiev, cranberry muffins and asparagus.
Carol and Jim take turns scolding Lily for her table man-
ners. Jim seems very uncertain of his surroundings, and his
discomfort makes me feel more at home. Although he has
been here two days longer, I feel he's the outsider, the rude
interloper. I hate his clothes and his mustache. I also hate
the way he snaps at Lily. She's not even his kid. I wink at
her across the table. Bunny announces she isn't going to eat
anything and makes good on her threat, though she filled
her plate to stop the argument. She's upset because her
mother yelled at her about the phone calls. The news is
on TV. A group in Boston is in front of a hospital protesting
abortion.

'Jim and I belong to a right-to-life group back home,'
Carol says.

'A woman should have the right to do whatever she
wants with her body,' Bunny says.

'No one has the right to murder the unborn.'

I find it annoying the way everyone bandies around the
concept of *rights*.

'It would be nice if you people were as concerned with
living women as you are with fetuses,' Bunny says.

'Murder,' Carol says. 'That's what you're talking about.'

'Is this dinner-table conversation,' Ginny asks.

Tory stands up and excuses herself, then leaves the
room.

'That was lovely, girls,' Ginny says. 'Tory's going into
the hospital on Monday.'

191

'Excuse me,' I say. 'I'll go see if she's all right.'

Tory's in her room, lying facedown on the bed. I sit beside her and stroke her hair. 'It's going to be all right.'

She flips over to face me. 'All right for you. You don't want children. You're glad about all of this.'

'That's not fair.'

'I wouldn't even be having these problems if it weren't for you. I'd be a mother already if it weren't for you.'

'We weren't ready yet. It would've been a mistake.'

'Carol is right. It's murder.'

'You don't believe that.'

Carol's inside the room before she knocks on the open door. She stands beside the bed. 'I don't mean to barge in,' she says. 'But I thought maybe I could be of help.' She lowers her ponderous form onto the bed. 'None of us is strong enough to bear his burden alone.'

'All of us are strong enough to bear the misfortunes of others,' Tory says.

'Jesus wants to lighten your load. All you have to do is ask.' Carol stretches out her hand to Tory, who examines it and its owner with mild distaste. 'Do you love Jesus, Tory?'

'Do I look like a necrophiliac to you?'

I expect Carol to be shocked, but her smile is indelible. 'You can run from Jesus, but you can't hide.'

Tory says, 'But can you get a restraining order, is what I want to know.'

The evening passes in the kitchen in front of the TV. The women are skilled at dividing their attention between the television and one another, so while never seeming to watch they will suddenly comment on the action on the screen. The conversation has a casual, intimate rhythm. I listen from outside the circle, a privileged observer. I enjoy studying Tory on her home ground, and am eager to pick up the family lore. I feel a renewed interest, seeing her in this context. More than bone structure and habits of speech, I can see aspects of character I was never quite able to bring into focus suddenly illuminated and framed in their genetic setting. I feel like someone whose appreciation of an artist has been based on a single painting but then is suddenly admitted to his studio.

My role of licensed connoisseur is compromised by the presence of Jim. Awkward and out of place, he butts into the conversation to ask who or what. He looks resentful, worried that a joke is being perpetrated at his expense. Mercifully, Jim heads up early after yawning pointedly at his wife. She tells him she'll be up soon. Bunny is up and down. At one point she disappears for most of a sitcom. I find myself sharing Ginny's anger at the old bastard who's stealing her youth.

Ginny keeps saying how nice it is to have everyone home, until, with her fourth drink, she begins to foresee the end of the reunion and slips into sullenness. 'Mary's been out every night since she got her license,' she complains to Carol and Tory. 'She's no company. She doesn't have time to sit down with her old mom. She's always coming or going, and everything's a big secret. She doesn't tell me anything. And then Bunny. She hates me because I don't want her to throw her life away.'

'She doesn't hate you,' Tory says impatiently.

'Of course she doesn't,' Carol says. 'She *loves* you. We *all* love you.'

Ginny looks at Carol through tears and says, 'Spare me this indiscriminate love. The trouble with you religious types is that you're promiscuous. Love, love, love. But then, you always *were* a cheap date.'

'Stop it,' Tory says. 'That's no way to talk to your daughter.'

'That's all right, Tory,' Carol says. 'I understand Mom's anger.'

'No you don't,' Ginny says, slapping her palm down on the table. 'You can't begin to understand my anger.'

I feel I should leave, but right now that would only make my presence more blatant.

'Between your sloppy el-you-vee and Tory's Ice Queen judgment, I'm dying for a little daughterly affection.' She shakes her head. 'What a brood. And Bunny. As if I need to be reminded about old leches and young bimbos.'

Ginny lights a cigarette. 'And where the hell is Mary? She's supposed to be in at eleven o'clock.' We all turn to the clock above the range: it says ten-forty. 'All right,' Ginny says, 'so she's got twenty minutes.' They all laugh at the same moment, like synchronized swimmers executing an abrupt, graceful maneuver, their anger dispersed.

'Do you think she's still a virgin?' Ginny asks suddenly.

'Of course she's a virgin,' Tory says.

'Mary's a sensible girl,' Carol says. 'She's not going to let herself be talked into anything.'

I remember Tory told me that Carol had her first abortion when she was fifteen.

'She's only sixteen,' Tory says.

194

'She's so cute,' Carol says.

'She is,' Ginny says.

Tory turns to me and says, 'Isn't she a cutie?'

I could get very inspired on this subject. Instead I just say, 'She sure is.'

Carol says, 'Remember that time she stuck the key in the electrical socket?'

At eleven o'clock Tory announces she's tired. 'You don't have to come to bed yet,' she says to me. I would like to stay up with the others, to sit quietly and listen to three women talk, but I say I'll come up with her. Ginny lets us share a room. Everyone kisses goodnight. Bunny, who has come back down, presses close enough for me to feel her breasts as she kisses me. Carol's breath smells chemically sweetened. Ginny folds me in a long, motherly hug. She says she's going up, too.

After she takes off her shirt, Tory points to the small protuberance on her left side. It is the size of a BB, only slightly darker than the surrounding skin. 'Do you know that this would have been enough evidence to convict me of witchcraft in the seventeenth century?' she says.

I do know, because she has told me several times, but I say, 'Really?'

'It's what they call an auxiliary nipple. A devil's teat. Proof that I've been suckling demons.'

'Rules of evidence have advanced a little since then,' I say cheerfully.

'Wouldn't it be strange if in former lives you were a prosecutor at the witch trials and I was a witch.'

'I'm on your side, Tory,' I say, putting my arms around

her. As her face disappears against my chest I see that she is looking not at me but at some region inside herself. 'Everything will be all right,' I say. I can still see the sadness in her eyes and mouth. 'We'll have children together.' Maybe I say it because I want to sleep with her sisters and I feel guilty about it, or because she thinks that like her father I'll leave and I'm afraid she's right.

Lying there after Tory has fallen asleep, I conjure up the image of Bunny and Tory sleeping side by side on this same bed, and think about how I felt then, how I wanted to crawl between them and have both. What I really imagined, seeing these two women who look so much alike, was a single woman who was Tory leavened with Bunny's careless grace. As I drift toward sleep, I superimpose Mary's face, which seemed to me in the liquor store parking lot to be fearless and flushed with sexual anticipation, and to that I add Carol's womb. Then I see Ginny alone in the bed in which the four of them had been conceived. And I think of my own mother, who is dead, and my father, whom I haven't seen in eight months, and imagine myself as a pinprick of life, floating whole in the dark, before all of these divisions and divorces and separations.

A NOTE ON THE AUTHOR

Jay McInerney is the author of six novels, *Bright Lights, Big City*, *Ransom*, *Story of My Life*, *Brightness Falls*, *The Last of the Savages* and *Model Behaviour*. He lives in New York and Nashville.

A NOTE ON THE TYPE

The text of this book is set in Berling roman, a modern face designed by K. E. Forsberg between 1951–58. In spite of its youth it does carry the characteristics of an old face. The serifs are inclined and blunt, and the g has a straight ear.

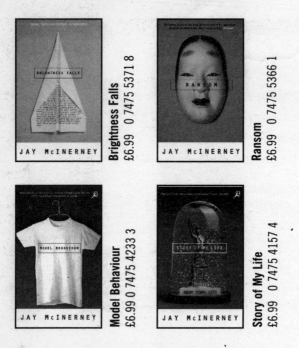